W9-BMD-044

TOXICOLOGY

Also by Jessica Hagedorn

Dogeaters

Danger and Beauty

Charlie Chan Is Dead: An Anthology of Contemporary Asian American Fiction (editor)

The Gangster of Love

Burning Heart: A Portrait of the Philippines (with Marissa Roth)

Dream Jungle

TOXICOLOGY

Jessica Hagedorn

VIKING

VIKING
Published by the Penguin Group
Penguin Group (USA) Inc., 375 Hudson Street,
New York, New York 10014, U.S.A.
Penguin Group (Canada), 90 Eglinton Avenue East, Suite 700,
Toronto, Ontario, Canada M4P 2Y3
(a division of Pearson Penguin Canada Inc.)
Penguin Books Ltd, 80 Strand, London WC2R 0RL, England
Penguin Ireland, 25 St. Stephen's Green, Dublin 2, Ireland
(a division of Penguin Books Ltd)
Penguin Books Australia Ltd, 250 Camberwell Road, Camberwell,
Victoria 3124, Australia
(a division of Pearson Australia Group Pty Ltd)
Penguin Books India Pvt Ltd, 11 Community Centre, Panchsheel Park,
New Delhi – 110 017, India
Penguin Group (NZ), 67 Apollo Drive, Rosedale, Auckland 0632,
New Zealand (a division of Pearson New Zealand Ltd)
Penguin Books (South Africa) (Pty) Ltd, 24 Sturdee Avenue,
Rosebank, Johannesburg 2196, South Africa

Penguin Books Ltd, Registered Offices:
80 Strand, London WC2R 0RL, England

First published in 2011 by Viking Penguin,
a member of Penguin Group (USA) Inc.

1 3 5 7 9 10 8 6 4 2

Publisher's Note

This is a work of fiction. Names, characters, places, and incidents either are the product of the author's imagination or are used fictitiously, and any resemblance to actual persons, living or dead, business establishments, events, or locales is entirely coincidental.

LIBRARY OF CONGRESS CATALOGING IN PUBLICATION DATA

Hagedorn, Jessica Tarahata, date.
Toxicology / Jessica Hagedorn.
p. cm.
ISBN 978-0-670-02257-1
ISBN export edition 978-0-670-02290-8
1. Neighbors—Fiction. 2. Women motion picture producers and directors—Fiction. 3. Women authors—Fiction. 4. Older women—Fiction. 5. Female friendship—Fiction. 6. City and town life—New York (State)—New York—Fiction. 7. Manhattan (New York, N.Y.)—Fiction. I. Title.
PS3558.A3228T69 2011
813'.54—dc22

2010035379

Printed in the United States of America
Set in Bembo and Bulmer MT
Designed by Alissa Amell

FOR THE GHOSTS

When something bad happens, sometimes you wanna be a part of it.

—VIOLET SMITH

La verdadera lucha es con el duende.

—FEDERICO GARCÍA LORCA,
from "Play and Theory of the Duende"

The true—struggle, fight, whichever you prefer—is with the duende.

—ELEANOR DELACROIX

TOXICOLOGY

OMG

It was Violet who texted Mimi and broke the news. Her message all in caps, to emphasize the importance and gravity of the situation. Fourteen-year-old Violet, of all people, had her little finger on the zeitgeist.

OMG MOM HES DEAD TURN ON CNN NOW!!!

Romeo Byron the He who was dead mysteriously and suddenly, the news of it traveling so swiftly that by the time Mimi got to East Third and First, a vigil was already in progress, media trucks lined up and the rubberneckers having a field day, a phalanx of cops guarding the entrance to Byron's brownstone, Mimi thinking that some of the younger rookies were probably fans of the moody star, thrilled to be at the epicenter but trying not to show it. So what if this took all night, so what if it was cold, so what if the crowd was growing bigger and kookier by the minute, so what if they weren't getting paid overtime, so what if the economy sucked, so what if the ME was stuck in traffic? This was history, a fucking for-real New York moment, *tragic and amazing*, and they—startled rookie cops fresh from the academy—were the chosen ones. Guarding the entrance to *his house*, privy to all the weird shit and rumors about him, what happened and why, who was in the joint when it happened, alla that. *Weird shit.* For example Johnny Depp may have been a houseguest, for example Chloë Sevigny stopped by the night before with Benicio and one of the Olsen twins, the really scuzzy one who's always photographed with a Venti-size Starbucks to-go clutched in her little hand. A cup no doubt filled with vodka. Or maybe that's Lindsay Lohan with the vodka. Or Jay-Z. Whatever, they were all his *friends.* Wait a sec. I heard that Romeo Byron had no friends. He may have been a sweet, salt-of-the-earth, give-you-the-bling-off-my-back kinda guy, but I heard the kid didn't have, didn't want or need, any friends.

Truth.

Mimi edged up to a dapper old man who looked like her father, Balthazar, might have looked, had he survived. Have they brought out the body? The old man sipped discreetly from a flask, dressed for the winter in a dark green trilby hat and a finely cut coat. Probably cashmere. He seemed amused by her question. Meat wagon hasn't gotten here yet, pretty lady. The firemen and EMS are inside, CSU, borough chiefs, more cops. Too many people, if you ask me. What're they all doing? Mimi asked. What do you think they're doing? The old man playful, sarcastic. I dunno, Mimi said. Interviewing witnesses? Swiping souvenirs to auction on eBay? Taking pictures of the body with their cell phones? The old man appraised Mimi with a hard, shrewd gaze. Eyes that had seen everything, yet friendly. And though he was a man well past seventy, it didn't stop him from flirting. Other big shots are on their way, he said. The commissioner for sure, maybe even the mayor. They all show up when someone high-profile dies and the dying stinks.

Excuse my asking, Mimi said, after a pause. You a retired detective or something? Maybe I am, the old man said. And you? Some kinda reporter or something? Mimi was about to lie, then decided against it and shook her head. Didn't think so, the old man said. You aren't dressed right. *No tienes frío?* The old man taking in the hatless head, gloveless hands, the ratty scarf carelessly wrapped around her neck, the inadequate jacket she wore over her jeans. I was in a rush, Mimi said. Had no idea how cold it was. The old man offered Mimi his flask. Mimi hesitated, sorely tempted. She had not eaten all day. Go ahead, the old man urged in a gentle voice. It will keep you warm. Mimi took the flask and drank. So, the old man said, after a long moment. You are one of the dead man's grieving fans?

She lost him in the swelling crowd. One minute the dapper, courtly old man was standing beside her, the next he was gone. His name, he'd told her at one point, was Mauricio Silva. Damn, Mimi thought. Why didn't I take Mauricio's picture? But instinct told her that Mauricio Silva would've refused.

Mimi tried to get closer to Romeo Byron's brownstone, but there were too many people in the way. Still, she had a great view of the wide stone steps leading up to the front entrance, where the tense cops stood guard. The fans had left their humble offerings along each side of the curved wrought-iron railings: flowers from the local deli, flickering votive candles, teddy bears clutching satin lollipops in their paws, little airplane bottles of vodka, heart-shaped Mylar balloons, handwritten farewell poems tucked into envelopes addressed to "R.B." Mimi wondered if there was some way she could steal the life-size cardboard cutout that some fan had propped up against the façade of the building. Romeo posed as Doppelganger, a smirk on his ghoulishly made-up face. Doppelganger was the lead character in the soon-to-be-released movie of the same title. Based on a popular manga series, the ode to violence had cost $200 million to make and was shot on location in New Zealand and Morocco. Sweet Romeo Byron had never played such a freaky villain as this. *I am your mirror. I am your dreams.* There was much advance buzz, audacious sneak peeks on YouTube. Mimi knew that the movie was going to be horrible and crass and brilliant. And now that he was dead, she, along with Violet and thousands of other people, could not wait to see it.

Mimi took the Flip video out of her bag. The camera so compact and unobtrusive it fit in the palm of her hand. She glanced around. Violet, no doubt, had cut school. She was somewhere in the vicinity, somewhere in that milling crowd with her posse of feral friends. Kenya, Charlie, Omar,

Bethanne. The party in full swing. Mimi began shooting, aiming the lens at the anonymous-looking building, panning across the teddy bears and candles and flowers, the bereft fans, the cops, the reporters. A tear fell. Then another. Mimi kept shooting, disgusted with herself. She was not one of his tweeting stalkers, those pathetic scholars of Romeology who made it a point to know where he lived, who he fucked, the kinds of books and music he loved, the kinds of muffins and dope he consumed for breakfast. There was no reason for her to cry. People like Romeo Byron messed up and died young all the time. It came with the territory.

She agreed with the zealous fans on one thing. Romeo Byron was not afraid to go *there.* To watch him act was a joy, scary and moving, almost embarrassing. Mimi's gaze wandered up to the dark row of windows on the top floor. Where his bedroom was supposedly located. The blinds were drawn. There was a hush and a stillness to the building, as if it were frozen in time. Mimi thinking, The entire nation is already so fucking depressed. *I'm so fucking depressed.* What if Romeo's death were just another prank or hoax? She imagines the blinds pulled up by unseen hands. The lights coming on. Romeo Byron standing at a window, smiling that ambivalent smile of his. She imagines an angry, disappointed fan shouting from the street: *We got punk'd!*

Believe. Romeo Byron was the actual name on his birth certificate. He was an only child. Father a physicist, denied tenure at Stanford, sixty-one years old and in the early stages of dementia when Romeo was born. Mother who, except for an exquisite, limited-edition, hand-stitched chapbook, was an unpublished poet and short-story writer, about to turn forty. Imagine the shock that she had managed to conceive after all those years. Imagine the awkward delight, the shame and the dread. Mimi remembers Violet reading something online (TMZ? maybe TMZ) about Romeo coming home from school to discover his mother hanging from a beam in the master bedroom. He was nine years old.

There was a housekeeper and a personal assistant who came and went seven days a week, also a sometime girlfriend who was pregnant with Romeo's baby. She was a nobody who lived in Paris and planned to raise the child as a single parent, according to Violet and *Entertainment Tonight*. Whether any of it was true, for all intents and purposes Romeo Byron lived alone in the three-story brownstone. Its proximity to the Hells Angels clubhouse had been a major selling point, according to the interview real-estate broker Jill Stockhausen later gave to *Dateline NBC*. Romeo liked the idea that the Hells Angels were right across the street. He went on about karma and synergy, Stockhausen said. Stuff that made no sense to me. I mean, what *synergy*? Romeo was wussy about motorcycles, and frankly, those guys made him nervous. Yet he was attracted, Stockhausen said. She also said, with a soft, self-deprecating laugh, We were in the same acting program at Juilliard. He was my friend.

Romeo was murdered by drug dealers, was molested as a child, was bipolar, was genius, exhausted, brokenhearted, had stopped taking his meds, had mixed up his meds, had chronic insomnia, had committed suicide, had simply fucked up big time, had OD'd.

The medical examiner finally arrived. *At five in the afternoon, exactly five in the afternoon!* Mimi checked her cell. Well, actually, it was more like 5:49 P.M. She slowly elbowed her way through the throng. They could be bringing him out at any second. Him the corpse, the shell of Romeo Byron. The seconds and minutes ticked by. The hours. Mimi was amazed by her willingness to stand there and wait. She and the throng so mesmerized by that nondescript front door, so fucking patient, so fucking rapt and coiled tight, not wanting to miss a thing. To pass the time, Mimi shot footage of the rather quaint Hells Angels clubhouse of orange bricks, zooming in on the black steel door with its gaudy mural of demons, skulls, and yellow-orange flames. Mimi thinking, *How very Halloween.* Yet it evoked a certain power. Mimi realized that there was no reason for her to be surreptitious about filming. Not a grizzled Hells Angel or a Harley chopper in sight, which was actually quite disappointing.

Night had fallen, and it was colder than ever. A young girl in a skimpy Juicy Couture sweat suit stood in the middle of the street, trembling and disoriented. *O Romeo, Romeo, wherefore art thou Romeo?* she wailed, possessed. Mimi pointed the camera at her.

The front door was held open by a cop. The EMS guys wheeled Romeo's body out on a metal gurney, trying their best to ignore the circus of downtown freaks and paparazzi gathered outside. Hundreds of cameras went off at once, flashbulbs popping like gunfire, lighting up the night. Random sighs curses and moans from the throng. Love, Mimi thought. One love, and why not? Him zipped inside a black plastic bag. A small, insignificant lump that jiggled on the gurney as the nervous EMS guys hurried to get everything into the waiting van and drive away. Yo, that wuz some sad, sick shit, one of them will say later to his wife.

That's a prop! A decoy! Not him! The Juicy Couture girl rocked and keened. Mimi kept the camera on her. *Give me my Romeo, and when I shall die, / Take him and cut him out in little stars, / And he will make the face of heaven so fine . . .* The Juicy Couture girl fell on her knees in the street, closed her eyes, and clasped her hands in prayer. Her lips were moving, but the camera wasn't picking up any sound. Mimi tried getting closer to her, but a cop got in the way. Another cop started yelling through a bullhorn. Come on, people! Move it! Go home! The party's over! There's nothing for you here! Mimi put the Flip video back in her bag and started walking west, exhausted and drained by the histrionic displays of emotion. The walk would do her good. Wouldn't it be sweet to run into someone, someone she knew and liked and trusted, and maybe get high? Who was in town? Who was feeling compassionate and magnanimous, who wanted to share? Mimi turned up her collar and walked a little faster. She could feel it now. The cold.

Eat the Gun

She slept until the next afternoon. Don't be afraid, Romeo Byron said in her dream. The ceiling and floor and walls of her bedroom were swarming with caterpillars. He stood in the doorway, edgy and distracted, completely naked. His long, stringy blond hair was damp. A gun dangled from his hand. Mimi tried to say, I had a good time at your vigil, but the words wouldn't come. Was she lying down or sitting up? Her body a Flip video, aimed at a burning star.

What I'd give for sardines, Romeo said with a sigh. Bread and peppers and sardines!

You gonna shoot me? Mimi asked.

Prop. I'm doing *Hamlet* at the Delacorte.

Romeo lay down under the covers and closed his eyes, the gun still clutched in his hand. Mimi straddled his sleeping body and yanked a caterpillar out of his left ear. Romeo opened his eyes and grinned. Thanks, he said. You're an angel.

Mimi felt the sudden urge to fuck him. Or bite his neck and draw blood. A secret she must keep from Violet. OMFG, Violet!

And for such a small boy, you've got a humongous head.

A movie star's head, Romeo snapped. His tone became desperate. I'm hungry, woman. Please. Help me out.

Eat the gun, Mimi said.

She woke up drenched in sweat, yet cold. The blankets were on the floor. Was the beast still alive? She hated the gloom of winter and felt the faint beginnings of an old, familiar dread. It always started the same way—the utter aloneness, a queasiness in her gut. Then the endless, terrifying litany of what-ifs. Mimi forced herself to get out of bed and turned the lights on. Better. In the bathroom she peed, then washed her face and quickly brushed her teeth, avoiding the mirror above the sink. She turned the lights on in the narrow, windowless kitchen and tried not to look at the beast lying in the box. The beast was lying very still. Mimi brewed a small pot of Bustelo for herself. She emptied the pot into a large mug and drank it, black. The coffee was strong and made things worse. She ran back into the bathroom just in time to throw up in the toilet. She felt lost, still in her dream. How could she have slept so late? She rinsed her mouth out and brushed her teeth a second time, trying not to puke again. What she needed now, what she really needed now was—

Back in the kitchen, she opened the refrigerator door. Contemplated the word *fame* while pouring herself the last bits of precious fuel from her stash in the freezer. On the rocks, garnished with a twist, the premium blend tasted dangerous and smooth. She relished each oily sip of her cocktail, fought the urge to guzzle it down. Cost of gas rising. Prices the highest they'd ever been on the day the young actor lay down and died, the exact same day Mimi filched the shipping box from the recycling bin in the basement and made a bed for the dying animal. The dead actor was famous. The dying animal was not.

No product to be found in all of Manhattan or Brooklyn, or any other borough, for that matter. Mimi considered knocking on the old woman's door. Eleanor was never without. Mimi licked her lips, fought the urge to visit the old woman, and moved into the living room. She switched on a lamp. Better. Definitely. Light swept the dread and the what-ifs into a dusty little corner and made it all better. She flipped open her cell, scrolled down to reread the old texts from Bobby.

Bitch b cool

Yr palz 2 fuckin bad.

Bad bad not good bad.

Dnt panic. Go 2 Picasso.

Seconds later he had texted her again before disappearing from her life.

I wl miss u.

Bobby random about which words to abbreviate and which to spell out. Bitch, cool, panic, *Picasso.* Code for Eleanor. Code that made no sense to Mimi. Eleanor's a writer, Mimi had argued. Why Picasso? Why not call her Proust?

Best code's got no logic to it. Bobby had said. The fuck's Proust?

French dude. Wrote all this shit without getting out of bed.

Bobby chuckled. Sounds too much like Eleanor, babe.

Before Bobby left town, jumped ship, went out for cigarettes, whatever you want to call it, he and Mimi had been summoned to Ingrid and Badr's loft on Walker Street. The loft was vast and sleek and chilly, more of a showcase for their eclectic art collection than a home. It was where Mimi had first glimpsed Yvonne Wilder's work. Three small paintings of a child's face from slightly different angles, in dark shades of green and pink. Eyes squeezed shut, mouth wide open.

Wow, Mimi remembered saying.

It's one of Wilder's very early pieces, Ingrid had said, coming up from behind. She calls it *Three Studies for My Son's Head*. Beautiful, no?

And ugly, Mimi remembered saying.

Badr had flown in just that afternoon, carrying product from his various associates in Barcelona. Ingrid seemed excited. Come around nine, she'd said. Don't be late. She and Badr were all of a sudden interested in doing business with Bobby. But why? Mimi wondered. They certainly didn't need the money; they were swimming in it. Bobby was flattered by the louche couple's attention. Plus, he was intrigued by the sensuous, older, blasé Ingrid, Mimi knew. Ever since the night the four of them got wasted and ended up in Ingrid and Badr's plush, enormous bed, she knew. There was nothing Mimi could do. It was her fault that Bobby had met them in the first place.

They remind me of Komodo dragons, she once said to him. You know Komodos, right?

You think I'm so ghetto, Bobby had said, with a little laugh.

WHAT.

Just like your pals Ingrid and Badr. Gets them off. Gets *you* off.

Where—Mimi sighed—is this going?

Wherever you'd like it to go, Bobby said.

I was talking about Komodo dragons. *Monitor lizards.*

Their saliva's red, Bobby said. You know that, right?

Ingrid and Badr were connoisseurs of gore. Chan-wook Park. Dario Argento. Eli Roth. They signed on to invest in Mimi's film *Blood Wedding,* brought in at the eleventh hour by Ivan and Matthieu, Mimi's executive producers.

Certain friends have come to the rescue, Matthieu had announced over lunch at Pastis. He and Ivan were feeling expansive and footing the bill.

Dear friends, Ivan added. Old friends.

What took them so long? Mimi was playing with her salad and in a vile, ungrateful mood.

Ivan gave her a frosty smile. You're welcome, he said.

The exotic couple's investment was substantial, and Mimi—in spite of herself—grew to feel increasingly dependent. When she was done shooting and without the knowledge of Ivan and Matthieu, Mimi made an appointment to see Ingrid and Badr at their loft. She was anxious and overwhelmed by her need for money. Rent, the combined MasterCard and American Express bills that needed paying down (twelve grand and change, 19 percent interest), the IRS balance (thirty-eight hundred) still owed for 2001—a truly shitty year—that needed paying off, as well as the five thousand she had originally borrowed from Violet's father, Dash, so she could move. Of course we will help, Badr assured her. Yes, Ingrid said. We like to help. Can we keep this confidential? Mimi asked, trying not to show her humiliation.

They loaned her fifteen thousand dollars. Will this do? Ingrid handed Mimi the check. Mimi glanced at it in disbelief. Not exactly everything she needed, but *wow.* Thank you, Mimi said after a pause. This is more than I— Ingrid and Badr nodded and smiled in sympathy. Mimi detected a hint of superiority in their expressions of concern. I'll pay you back as soon as the movie— She hesitated, again overcome with shame. She was about to say something about *distribution,* but Badr put up his hand.

No pressure, Badr said. We understand.

Artists lead brave, difficult lives, Ingrid said. And we love them for it.

Just keep making your movies, Badr said.

Just keep making your movies. Mimi had managed to finish only one. And had decided never to call herself an artist. Thinking of yourself as an artist got you into trouble. Just ask her ex, Dashiell Smith, Mr. Unrealized Dreams. Whose bland last name Mimi had long ago conveniently adopted. She played along with Ingrid and Badr. If they needed her to be an artist, then she would be. Whatever they needed to believe was okay with Mimi back then.

She started with noble intentions, telling herself she would get rid of as much debt as she could. Mimi paid off the IRS but ended up sending Dash only half of what she owed him. She sent a two-thousand-dollar payment to AmEx and absolutely nothing to MasterCard. Mimi then bought Violet a North Face for the coming winter. What was left of the loan, she transferred into her online savings account.

Badr was eager for Bobby to sample the coke from Spain. A little too eager, Mimi thought. For Badr was suave and cool, never eager. Ingrid, too. Suave and cool, lurking close by Badr's side. Mimi remembered trying to think of an excuse to leave, remembered praying for her cell phone to ring while asking herself, Why doesn't Violet call when I need her to call? She remembered not saying much of anything, Ingrid putting on music, Bobby watching intently as Badr chopped away at the heap of tiny, dingy rocks laid out on the glass table, Bobby grinning that dangerous grin as he said to Badr, Your shit looks dirty, man.

Badr looking at him. Not saying anything, the razor in his hand.

You're being paranoid, Ingrid murmured. We expected more out of you.

Bobby grabbed Mimi's hand.

Should she erase Bobby's text messages? No, not yet. She needed the instant replay, to keep savoring his last words to her. She was still angry with him for disappearing; she missed him terribly, deeply. It surprised her how much. It was a thunderbolt-and-lightning-strike sort of moment when they first met at a dismal midtown karaoke bar called Nightingale. Mimi's brother, Carmelo, had called earlier that day to invite her to drop by for a song and a drink. A song *and* a drink? Mimi had said. She had to laugh. Thanks, but no thanks. I'm busy.

Carmelo was a sucker for karaoke, had been known to get onstage after one or two beers to croon the corny seventies shit that he loved.

"You Are the Sunshine of My Life." "We've Only Just Begun." Donna Summer's drama queen disco version of "MacArthur Park." Their parents' music. Don't give me that busy shit, Carmelo said. You're always giving me that busy shit. Mimi remembered losing it on the phone. Listen, Melo—I'm trying to get a little movie made, and I don't have time for fucking karaoke. On top of that, I'm broke. And on top of alla that, Violet's decided to go live with her father!

It's my birthday, Carmelo had said quietly. So indulge me, okay? And quit feeling sorry for yourself. Your fucking movie will get made, and Violet will be back. And on top of alla that? The drinks are on me.

Your birthday. Fuck. I'm sorry, Melo. I forgot.

She was not planning to stay long. Carmelo was sitting at the bar, having a discreet chat with some guy when Mimi walked in. You're late, he teased. He was drinking something very grown-up, like scotch or bourbon. Mimi could tell he was lit. The guy sitting next to Carmelo had smoky hazel eyes. He was staring at her. Mimi's tone was confrontational. *Do I know you?* Now you do, Bobby had said. Wanna be in a movie? Mimi asked him. Aware that her brother was sitting there, watching them flirt. But no matter. Carmelo was lit and ready to sing. He couldn't care less if his younger sister was being too slutty or forward. Depends, Bobby had said. Whose movie we talkin' about?

Mine, Mimi answered.

She went home with him that night. She had not been with anyone since breaking up with Dash and began to shake. Sex with Bobby felt strange and raw. Everything strange and raw and new. They spent a lot of time fucking and getting high. The weeks stretched into months. Mimi an emaciated, glorious mess. Unable to keep food down, diarrhea constant, all she could focus on was getting through *Blood Wedding*. And Bobby. O the guilt. Violet refusing to visit, to return her pleading calls. The animal Violet left behind when she moved in with her father would go for days without being fed.

Days keep flying by. So much work, so little money, nothing to do. Get a job, Mimi. Any job. Keep yourself busy. You aren't a total nobody, after all. *Blood Wedding* still fresh in people's minds. There was that big-shot professor from NYU. What was her name? Judith. Judith Wexler. Author of a huge, scholarly tome that critics were forever referencing, entitled *The Metaphysics of Cinema Violence* (Illustrated, 642 pages, Oxford University Press). Mimi had never heard of it. She later saw a copy of the book on Eleanor's shelf. Made a note to borrow it and never did.

Judith Wexler brought her graduate students to an early screening of *Blood Wedding* and introduced herself to Mimi afterward. Your film is incredibly female, incredibly Catholic. Disturbing, Judith Wexler had said, her handshake vigorous. Mimi kept silent.

I mean that as a compliment, Judith Wexler said.

I wasn't sure, Mimi said.

Let's have coffee or a drink sometime. Judith Wexler handed Mimi her card before walking away.

If Mimi could just find the damn card, she'd sit down and e-mail Judith Wexler right then and there, ask if there were teaching positions for people like her, people with special skills—female *and* Catholic—who had dropped out of college. Maybe an artist-in-residence, prestigious visiting-lecturer position, like the one Eleanor's painter girlfriend Yvonne had held for years at Vassar. Yvonne had been paid a lot of money to train it up to Poughkeepsie once a semester, give a talk on art history or whatever damn subject she wanted to talk about, have dinner with a select group of students and faculty, and train it back to Manhattan the next afternoon.

Should Mimi address Judith Wexler as "Professor Wexler" or adopt a more casual, breezier tone that didn't reek of desperation? ("Hi, Judith— We met at a screening of *Blood Wedding* two or three years ago, blah-blah-blah, etc. etc.") Eleanor would be glad to help her compose the e-mail. All Mimi had to do was knock on the old witch's door. But if all else failed and Mimi lost her nerve, there was always the Learning Annex or Gotham Writers' Workshop. Everything You Need to Know About Writing and Making an Indie Movie, Taught by an Expert. Depressing, but this was no time to be choosy.

It was not Mimi's style to feel sorry for herself. At least she had a couple more months left of her Ida Lupino Fellowship. The Ida was bestowed annually to five women filmmakers in the early stages of their career, chosen from a nationwide pool of nominees. Mimi had burst out laughing when the surprise phone call came, informing her that she'd won. Thirty-five hundred fifty-two dollars deposited in her checking account on the twenty-ninth of every month. Soon coming to an end.

The beast cried out in pain. Mimi tried not to flinch. She lit up one of those girlie Cuban cigars, a cherished souvenir from Bobby's many clandestine trips to Bobby-wouldn't-say-where. Even after all this time, the cigar tasted fresh. She ignored the animal's sporadic cries and stared out the window at the high-rise luxury-loft condo being built across the street. Each floor starting at six point six. Rooftop gym, spa, pool, garage, natch. Doorman, valet service, twenty-four-hour concierge, no-brainer. The architect was famous and Dutch.

Most of the sky and the Hudson River were now blocked from view. But so what? Mimi had always avoided looking at the river; it reminded her of too many other bodies of water and the terrifying, greasy oceans beyond. The beast was wheezing now. She heard it clearly, even from the living room. Mimi hated how it made such sad, awful, hurting sounds. One shimmering drop left in the humming fridge; take it slow and easy, Mimi. And speaking of fame, just like that most famous of famous Lorca poems about death— Mimi glanced at the clock on the wall. *At five in the afternoon. / . . . exactly five in the afternoon . . .* Lorca's hypnotic lament conjured the image of a young matador being gored, then eaten by some ancient Minotaur, conjured the image of the helpless, wheezing beast in the kitchen. Five in the afternoon and already dark as midnight.

Mimi took another hit off the dainty cigar before stubbing it out in an ashtray. She wondered why she couldn't remember any other lines from Lorca's poem. Five in the afternoon. At exactly five in the afternoon! You're such a drama queen, Mimi. Mimi It's All About Me-Me! Why the tears? You don't know any matadors. You never knew poor, dead Romeo Byron.

The animal crawled into the living room and emitted a long howl, shining eyes fixed on her.

I can't help you, Mimi said.

Mimi scooped up the limp, dehydrated animal. There was a time it wouldn't have been as easy. Now the animal felt wet and sticky and weighed nothing. She could not bear to look at it but carried the creature into her bedroom and—as gently as she could—lowered it on the bed. She snatched a blanket off the floor and tucked it around the animal's body. Enough to warm the beast, to make it feel snug and protected, but not to cover it in any way. She was careful about that. Something had happened when it was very young, for the beast reacted violently to being confined. It did not move, but its eyes were alert. Or so Mimi thought. I can't help you, Mimi said. But you're welcome to die here.

She was the squeamish type. Never mind the low-budget slasher films she watched with such glee and dreamed of making. You've seen the trailers. Supermodels trapped in desolate hostels in the Black Forest. Trembling jocks strapped down and slowly eviscerated by melancholy sadists. Genius scenarios. Her ex did not approve of her tastes and ambitions. When he got drunk and loose, Dash used to say to anyone who'd listen, Next time you invite Mimi to a dinner party? Watch the way she suddenly stops eating. Watch the way she flings her knife and fork, aiming straight for your face. The cutlery flung with such fucking *élan*!

Mimi went back to the living room, sat down at her computer, and Googled Romeo Byron. The blogosphere was humming. The online bulletin boards and chat rooms. DISCUSS. SHARE YOUR

THOUGHTS. *Sad. Tragic actor guy. So young! RIP. How could you? Oh, man. You were the source of our national pride.* LIKELY A SUICIDE OR ACCIDENTAL OVERDOSE. The headlines a jumble of contradictions. Mimi turned on the TV. This is not officially a crime investigation, Romeo Byron's lawyer was saying to Anderson Cooper. This is a death investigation. Apparently Romeo had a standing appointment with his tantric masseur. Apparently it was neither the housekeeper nor the personal assistant but the tantric masseur who discovered Romeo's naked, lifeless body on the bed. Apparently the tantric masseur had a key. Apparently the tantric masseur, carrying an umbrella and a set of keys, slipped out the side exit and hailed the first available taxi before the cops arrived. A search was on for the young man, one Jimmy from Cartagena.

Mimi switched to NY1. Clips from last night's spontaneous vigil were being shown. She hoped for some glimpse of herself in the crowd, hoped for a glimpse of Violet and her pals. The Juicy Couture girl was being cuffed and led away. A Hells Angel sporting a long, silver ponytail turned and muttered something to the camera, which was bleeped. We're here to bear witness, a solemn young man in a New York University varsity jacket said to reporter Vivian Lee. That's the least we can do for Romeo.

AKA Picasso

Mimi waited until the sun went down, until she was sure the animal was not dead but merely asleep. She threw on the long coat—the extravagant, hand-stitched Beguelin that looked so fabulously beat-up—over her jeans. The coat was a consolation gift to herself, the coat she couldn't really afford but what the hell. The shoulder bag, too. Another hand-stitched indulgence that Mimi had purchased two years ago and was still paying off. In defiance of the weather, she headed out the door in her flip-flops.

In the hallway she found Picasso wandering in her bulky chenille bathrobe, a hundred-dollar bill rolled up in her fist. A beautiful coincidence, Mimi thought. Synergy! Karma! Whatever!

You okay, Eleanor? Mimi asked. Then: I'm dry. Maybe you can help me out.

Picasso the old woman stared back at her, uncomprehending. Or pretending.

Eleanor?

I was thinking all day about the boy.

What boy? Mimi forced herself to sound polite, to stand still.

Romeo Byron. It's distressing. I've been distressed all day, thinking about that kid killing himself!

I was there.

What do you mean, you were *there*?

Soon as I heard, I went down to where he lived, Mimi said. Shot footage of them carrying his body out. I can show it to you later, if you want.

Eleanor was silent.

You know they're saying this whole thing might've been an accident?

There are no fucking accidents in this fucking glorious universe, and you of all people should know that! Eleanor quickly pulled herself together. Affected a casual and nonchalant tone. *Mind running an errand for me, dear?*

I'm late for a production meeting, Mimi said, wondering why she couldn't just tell Eleanor the truth.

I used to work the graveyard shift, Eleanor said. At one of those big law firms.

Yes, I know. *Before you got famous,* Mimi thought. She moved to the elevator and pressed the "down" button, praying it would come quickly so she could escape. Mimi knew she was being foolish, that she should put on her best face and act nice. She took a deep breath and tried again. I'm having an energy crisis, Eleanor. Think you can help me out?

Eleanor prattled on. Those big law firms with four or five names attached—I can't remember which one, but they're still in business. We were mostly women working that shift. Typing, proofing, revising. They sent us home by taxi every night. Well, actually it was the crack of dawn by the time we clocked out, but still dark. Not safe.

Those were the days, Mimi muttered, furious.

I have no idea what you mean, the old woman said. Those were the days? What the fuck do you mean?

I was commiserating with you, Eleanor. Jeez.

You coming to my reading?

I wouldn't miss it for the world.

I haven't done a public thing in ages, Eleanor said. Not sure I'm up to the scrutiny and the schadenfreude.

Don't be silly. You'll knock 'em dead.

Please. Spare me the platitudes.

Mimi pressed the "down" button a second, then a third time. Fucking elevator—

This Volga. It's some sort of dive, isn't it?

You should be flattered. Even What's-His-Name can't get a reading there.

I don't understand.

Philip Roth. The Volga doesn't bother with people like Philip Roth.

I don't think he does readings in bars. Or readings, period. And certainly not in Red Hook! I don't know if I've been to Red Hook more than once in my life.

Point is, you're gonna love it, Eleanor. You can bask in the glow of your fans' adoration.

Do you mind escorting me to the reading? I'll talk myself out of it if I have to go alone. You know I will.

What about asking Coco Schnabel?

I'd rather shoot myself.

Mimi headed toward the stairs. But you've been such a bitch to me, Eleanor. Why should I escort you?

Your feet, Eleanor said.

What about them?

Why aren't you wearing shoes? It's supposed to snow and rain, isn't it?

I dunno, Eleanor. Maybe it is.

Bitch, the old woman cackled. She held out the grubby hundred-dollar bill. Maybe later, on your way home? Beefeater. Camel Lights. I'll be up.

Mimi snatched the money from her. I'll do you the favor just this once, okay? I'll be back kinda late. Way late. Don't start buggin' on me.

Thank you, Mimi.

Mimi started down the stairs.

Eleanor yelled after her. Midnight! Crack of dawn! You hear me? You know I'm up. I'm always up!

Mimi laughed in spite of herself. No need to shout—Coco Schnabel might call the cops. See that, Eleanor? You're already buggin'.

If she held on to that hundred-dollar bill too long, who knew what might happen? On her way to catch the first of two trains to Woodside, Mimi decided it was best to get Eleanor's little errands over with. Spirits Rising was the cutesy name of one of the many new, cozy establishments that had suddenly sprouted up all over the neighborhood. Inside the tiny, cluttered shop, a pair of six-foot, whippet-thin Russian beauties and a handsome, platinum-haired man were in the midst of a festive wine tasting. The beauties were giddy and talking very loud in charming, heavily accented English. They barely glanced at Mimi as she carefully wended her way around them and headed for the display of various rare and exotic gins. If I can help you find anything, said the handsome man. Mimi guessed he was the proprietor.

Beefeater? Mimi asked.

Limited shelf space, the handsome man said, with a withering smile. Sorry. He turned his unwavering attention back to the waiting beauties as Mimi made her exit.

She found Eleanor's brand at another place closer to the Eighth Avenue station, this one a straight-up, no-frills liquor store run by a morose Korean and a morose younger man who looked to be his son. Eleanor's cigarettes Mimi picked up at Duane Reade, along with a second pack she bought for herself, thank you very much, Eleanor. Her mood was lifting. First thing tomorrow she'd make an appointment with Ivan and Matthieu and ask—no, *beg*—them for more money so she could pay the bills and start working on a new script. She hoped they weren't out of town. Lately they were always out of town, and they were slow—really fucking slow—about returning phone calls or responding to e-mails. A couple of real smug assholes, they were. But hey, they had come through in the past, and Mimi simply had to shed all that negative energy simmering in her dark heart and fucking transcend. Just business, nothing personal. First thing tomorrow and that one little phone call to those hedge-fund assholes could—*would,* for godsake, Mimi—change everything.

Emboldened by her optimistic better-luck-tomorrow fantasy, Mimi considered stopping by Wanda's on the way uptown to see if Bobby was hiding out there or really and truly gone. Maybe adrift in the Canary Islands with Ingrid and Badr. Bobby—master of random mindfucks—was capable of staging his own kidnap and death just to get a buzz going. His mother would gladly play accomplice—anything to keep her only son beholden, forever lost in her smothering, maternal orbit of love. Wanda Fontaine, soothsayer and cunning entrepreneur, was not one to mess with. She had taught Bobby everything about the business. How to be frugal, how not to trust anybody. Wanda was no doubt one of the lucky few in Manhattan with a huge reserve of fuel stashed away for the lean, hard times. Times such as now. Mimi hurried past the Minuit Houses, the Soviet-style, middle-income housing project where Bobby grew up. Tried not to think of her cravings, or Eleanor's considerable change stuffed in her wallet. She had to make it to Queens in one piece, without humiliating herself.

It began to drizzle, lightly at first. Then came torrents of gray, icy rain. Her toes were turning blue. Mimi carefully made her way down the slippery, cracked steps of the subway station. The kid huddled by the bank of MetroCard vending machines was roused from her stupor. A rust-colored mutt with a faded blue bandanna tied around its neck lay by her feet. *Spare change.* The kid thrust the requisite Styrofoam cup at Mimi, but the flat, halfhearted tone of her voice implied she expected nothing in return. Mimi peered intently at the very young girl, trying to make out who was hiding under the baggy hooded sweatshirt. Maybe Violet?

Violet was capable of crazy runaway shit like this, but the dog . . . The dog wasn't her style. What Mimi saw as she stepped closer was a homely moon face mapped by acne scars and elaborate piercings.

My dog could use some food, lady.

Mimi dug around in her bag. What about you?

Whatever, the kid said. Mimi dropped a twenty-dollar bill in the Styrofoam cup. Thank you, Eleanor.

God Sends Me to Speak Boldly to You

Carmelo opened the door, holding the cell to his ear. I forgot what a drag the 7 train can be, Mimi said by way of greeting. Her older brother looked surprised and not entirely pleased to see her standing in the doorway, haggard and drenched. Uh-huh, Carmelo murmured into the phone. Uh-huh. He stepped aside as Mimi entered the apartment. Man, he sighed. I'm really sorry to hear this, man. Mimi's curiosity was immediately piqued, but she feigned indifference and glanced at the newspapers and magazines piled around the living room. The hoarding that had started up again, after Brenda left. The *Onion*, the *Nation*, *Art in America*, *Rolling Stone*, *Maxim*, *US Weekly*, the *Advocate*, *InStyle*, *W*, *Portfolio*, the *Brooklyn Rail*, the *Filipino Reporter*, *amNewYork*. Salvaged from Starbucks, subway trains, and trash cans or bought when he had money. Carmelo's taste in reading material knew no bounds. It was the thing Mimi couldn't help but admire and love about her brother's collecting mania. The What the Fuck I Read Anything and Everything Mellow Carmelo. And somewhere buried in the shambles of his apartment were the 9/11 editions of the *New York Times*, the *Wall Street Journal*, and *El Diario La Prensa*.

Whatchu gonna do when they stop killing trees and publish everything online, Melo? Mimi once asked him.

He had laughed, totally unconcerned. Guess I'll open a museum.

There was other junk he hoarded. Cassettes of forgotten funk bands, martial-arts movies on VHS, mildewed self-help books left out on someone's stoop. FREE. HELP YOURSELF. And Carmelo did. Pretty soon the apartment would be filled from top to bottom with his treasures, making it almost impossible to enter or move around; pretty soon Carmelo would be forced to sleep in the bathroom, unless the stained bathtub became another repository; pretty soon Carmelo would be laid off from his latest job as a security guard at the Brooklyn Museum; pretty soon the landlord would come calling and have Carmelo evicted.

Mimi was relieved to see the out-of-tune upright piano still in its corner. There were piles of junk all over it, but Carmelo's prized possession had not yet been sold or bartered or given away. Which was always a hopeful sign. Maybe he'd sweep the junk off the piano, sit down, and simply start playing. A whacked-out, barely recognizable "Clair de Lune" or *Moonlight* Sonata, maybe. Carmelo could play that pretty Debussy and Beethoven shit since the age of five. Then maybe "Crepuscule with Nellie" by Thelonious Monk. Carmelo loved Monk's strangeness, loved the hesitant, anguished way he made music. Loved how Monk broke into a sweat after his performance was over and would sit there in silence, gazing down at the piano keys. Like he couldn't believe what had just happened. Her brother was complicated like Monk was complicated. Her brother had many shades.

Mimi made room for herself on the newspaper-strewn futon couch and sat. She watched her brother pace and listen hard to whoever was jabbering on the other end of the phone. She wanted him to hang up so she could ask him if he was playing again. She wanted to tell him about the poet on the 7 train. He was scrawny and pigeon-toed, wore ill-fitting clothes and a grimy Yankees cap in reverse on his head. But his gaze was steady, his voice clear and strong. *God sends me to speak boldly to you, ladies and gentlemen. For life is a mystery, and knowledge is the crown.*

She grew impatient and tried to catch her brother's attention, but

Carmelo kept ignoring her. His apartment was colder than she expected, and Mimi longed to take a couple of swigs from Eleanor's bottle of gin. The old girl probably wouldn't mind. Hopefully, the old girl also wouldn't mind and would find it amusing that Mimi had spent most of whatever money was left on herself.

The long walk from the subway stop to her brother's apartment had been a test. Mimi slipped off the flip-flops and studied her nasty feet. Was Melo going to acknowledge her misery or bother handing her a towel or a blanket? Not a chance. How she hated coming all the way to Woodside, hated the effort involved in visiting her brother. She found him even more depressing than she found herself. I'll call as soon as I have something, okay? Promise, Mimi overheard Carmelo saying. Who was he attempting to appease? No doubt a skank. Calling to beg for money, to be saved from some abusive ex-something-or-other. With the exception of Brenda, Carmelo was unbelievably stupid when it came to women. Always falling for manipulative skanks—preferably pale and tragic—who were genius at playing helpless. Don't worry, Carmelo said. I'll take care of it. He clicked off the cell and finally looked at his sister. Well, well, well. Howzit goin'?

You should move, Melo.

Say wha'?

You heard me, homeboy. This place is a dump, Mimi said. And getting here is always a fucking ordeal.

Aw, man. Why you gotta be such a snob? Didn't you read last Sunday's *Times*? This is an up-and-coming neighborhood, Carmelo said. *Vibrant. Diverse.* Best arepas outside of Bogotá.

Yeah, yeah, I know. The new Fort Greene.

Everything okay with your crib? he asked.

They'd love to get rid of me and put it on the market, if that's what you mean. I'm probably the only renter left, Mimi said. But fuck real estate. Who was that you were gabbing with?

Uncle Frank.

Mimi groaned in disgust.

Something bad happened to Agnes, Carmelo said.

Agnes? Mimi winced at the memory of her faraway and long-ago childhood playmate, a spindly girl the color of cinnamon. Wow. It's been ages, Mimi said. *Agnes.*

She was working without papers for this family way out in Jersey. Toms River or something. They brought her over with the promise of a green card.

Hard to believe anyone still falls for that crap, Mimi said.

You don't live in the real world.

Do you? Mimi sneered.

My brain isn't half as fried as yours, Carmelo said.

True dat, Mimi said.

Uncle Frank had no idea Agnes was here, Carmelo continued. Then last month he gets this phone call. Said she sounded like things were okay. She promised to call him again, but he hasn't heard from her since.

Mimi tried to conjure up an image of Agnes's face. The ragged crescent scar on her cheek. The wide nose and dark, alluring eyes. Cousin Agnes was a modest, funny girl, meek and compliant to the point of being dull. Mimi remembered playing with her when there was no one else to play with.

The people she worked for? They have money, Carmelo said. The husband's a doctor, the wife's a— I forgot. Anyway, they told Uncle Frank that Agnes was in cahoots with some pimp boyfriend, that she'd been stealing from them all along, which is why she ran away.

Can't they think up a better story? Mimi said.

Uncle Frank wants me to go see these people, said Carmelo.

This is too fucking much for me to process. I mean, you are aware that Romeo Byron was found dead yesterday, right? And now *Agnes*?

I fail to see the connection, Carmelo said.

This is too fucking much! Mimi shouted. Her heart beat wildly. She felt like passing out.

Carmelo shook his head slowly in disbelief. Goddamn. What're you on?

And of course the last thing that asshole Frank wants to do is deal with the cops! So he's asking you to—

Carmelo threw up his hands in frustration. You know what, Mimi? Uncle Frank's got his reasons.

I'm not judging him. Or you. Mind if I smoke?

Yes, Carmelo said. I do. After a pause he said, Those people in Jersey? The wife's, like, a distant relative of Uncle Frank's.

Mimi's first impulse was to laugh at the irony of it all, make a couple of quips about deranged families and hereditary genes, but she kept silent.

Carmelo waited before adding in a soft voice, Heavy, right?

Mimi nodded.

By the way, you look awful.

Thanks, Mimi said.

Sorry. I didn't mean—

Horseshit. Mimi changed the subject. So. Think maybe Agnes is no more?

Carmelo plopped down on top of the newspapers next to his sister. He stared at a wall of peeling paint and let out a deep breath. Then he buried his head in his hands. His shoulders began to shake. Mimi wondered why her brother was weeping and she was not. The poet on the train had ended his recitation by going up to each passenger and holding out his baseball cap. *Ladies and gentlemen, this concludes today's poetry session. Can you help me out with some change or a piece of wisdom?*

Mimi gave him change.

Carmelo ran a hand over his face. Why are you here?

I'm out of fuel, Mimi said. Thought you might lend a helping hand.

You've got nerve. Why don't you go ask those skeevy pals of yours? Sigrid and Abdul.

Mimi sighed. I'm afraid Ingrid and Badr have flown the coop. I have no one left to turn to but you, bro. And though you deeply despise me, you can't be rude. Remind yourself that we're orphans. That I'm all you've got. I know what you're thinking. That we can claim Frank, our so-called uncle who lives in a cemetery out there in fucking Colma. He's *family,* right?

Uncle Frank lives across from the cemetery, not *inside* the cemetery.

But family's what you're thinking. Family equals tragedies and obligations. Equals Melo and Mimi are not alone! Okay, I have to admit. Frank's our mother's whatever, Frank's blood. And so is—was?—that naïve Agnes girl. *Blood.* And if something fucking evil's gone down, what exactly can you do about it, Melo? How you gonna get started playing detective and get out to Bumfuck, New Jersey? You don't even own a *car.*

I'll rent one, her brother retorted.

Is Frank bankrolling this investigation? You live in a crumbling dump without any heat, Mimi reminded him. Cost of gas rising.

Furious, Carmelo leaped up from the couch and went into the bedroom. He emerged seconds later with a pair of thermal socks and a Disney World beach towel that had seen better days. He threw the socks and the towel at Mimi. If you came all the way out here just to hustle me for blow, then I think you can leave now.

Got any shoes I could borrow? Mimi knew that her attempt at a joke would fall flat as soon as she said it. She slipped the thick woolen socks on her feet and wrapped the large towel around her shoulders. Blood is blood, she said, but that gets real thin in the case of our beloved uncle, who ever since I can remember is always leaning on you . . . or me. Frank knows you can't say no to him and—

We owe Frank.

Don't fall for that debt-for-life shit, Melo. We are orphans and alone. Period. You have anything to drink?

There's ginger ale. And plenty of tap water.

Mimi took the bottle of Beefeater from her bag. Want some?

I'm taking a break, Carmelo said.

Since when?

Carmelo shrugged. Been almost three months.

Congratulations, Mimi said. I mean it.

You should take a break.

I will, Melo. I will. Mimi brought the bottle into the kitchenette. She rinsed out a jelly jar, threw in some grimy ice cubes and a healthy dose of Eleanor's gin. It occurred to her that the old woman might not be so amused after all. Mimi felt a twinge of guilt, but only a twinge. Her brother watched as she drank. This little bottle of gin actually belongs to my neighbor the writer lady, Mimi said. I'm her designated errand girl.

How is Eleanor?

Giving a reading at Volga. Thursday night. Gonna be hot.

Carmelo chuckled. Hot. Eleanor's, like, eighty years old.

So? Eleanor's a mythic presence. You should come.

Readings are boring.

But you're such a *reader,* Mimi said. Look at all these newspapers. These magazines and books!

Fuck off.

Promise you, bro—this will be an event. As you know, Eleanor writes dirty books and can be very entertaining when she chooses to be. The gin was making Mimi nauseous, but she poured herself more.

How's the new script coming along? Carmelo asked.

Practically writing itself, Mimi answered.

That's great.

Yeah, it is, Mimi said. Things are happening.

Like what?

Like what? Well. Tonight this homeless poet got on the 7 with me.

How'd you know he was homeless?

I knew.

And?

You believe in signs, Melo?

Carmelo stared at his sister.

This was definitely a sign, Mimi said. The guy starts rapping, and the rest of us are, like, feeling trapped and rolling our eyes and dreading what we're about to hear. Plus, he smelled kinda bad. But would you believe? His delivery—and the fucking poetry—they both were actually pretty good! I felt inspired, Melo. Really inspired.

Cool, Carmelo said, trying to sound convincing. Very cool.

I want to be just like him. I want to be as humble and brave as my homeless poet on the 7!

Carmelo told himself that if he really wanted to, he could make her stop. His breathless sister had the big mouth and the big game and thought *he* was the crazy one, but she was wrong.

Mimi started on her third round of gin and melted ice. I don't mean to be disrespectful by drinking in front of you, she said with a wistful smile. I can handle copious amounts of most toxins, so rest assured I won't get shitfaced. But by all means, Melo. If you want me to stop, if you need to call your sobriety sponsor or something—

Treatable. Incurable.

Six or seven months ago the man had called to invite her to read at Volga. Eleanor's first impulse was to hang up, but she stopped herself. With the coke pumping through her bloodstream, Eleanor suddenly felt curious, more open to being courted by the stranger on the phone. He introduced himself as Rajiv Gill. We'd be so honored to have you read for us, Eleanor. May I call you Eleanor?

Eleanor didn't respond.

We can only pay a modest honorarium, Rajiv continued after an awkward pause. But we'll wine and dine you. Take care of your local transport.

Does that mean the subway? I don't do subways.

Taxi. Or car service, if you prefer.

Fucking Mimi and her practical jokes. Did Mimi put you up to this? How'd you get my number?

I'm a friend of Benjy's.

Benjy . . . Benjy *who*?

There was another pause before Rajiv spoke again. Benjamin Wilder. Yvonne's—

GOT IT, Eleanor said. She took her time finding and lighting a cigarette. Don't you think that's rather cheeky of Ben to give you my number, Mr. Rajiv?

Our sincerest apologies if we've somehow offended—

How many are you?

I beg your pardon?

How many goddamn people are on the phone talking to me right now?

Just one, and that would be me.

Then I don't understand why you keep referring to yourself in the plural, Eleanor said before hanging up.

Rajiv called back before she had a chance to unplug the phone. Look, he said. I'm sorry for coming off like some pretentious son of a bitch.

Don't humiliate yourself, Mr. Rajiv.

We have a print-and-online magazine. Also called Volga.

I'm aware of it.

You are? That's wonderful. Really wonderful!

It's not bad.

Thank you. I'm . . . well, actually, I'm the founding editor. And what we—*I*—want to propose is to have a special issue devoted to your work. To be published after the reading, of course.

In spite of herself, Eleanor was flattered and intrigued. Why?

Because. You're a great writer and—

My work is challenging. And somewhat obscure.

Yes, but—

No one cares about books anymore. Least of all mine.

Oh, I don't think that's true at all, Rajiv said. Our readings are standing-room-only events. A whole new generation is going to be introduced to your work, which is a vital part of Volga's mission.

Eleanor groaned.

Your books will be on sale, of course, and—

You mean the ones still in print, Eleanor said, instantly regretting it. Thinking, How loathsome and self-pitying I've become.

After the reading's done, we'll set you up at a little table so you can—

I know what happens, Eleanor said. Shifty-eyed men show up, shoving bound galleys and first editions in your face. They demand your signature, walk away, and peddle the stuff on eBay!

Rajiv chuckled softly. So will you do it?

She had said yes and wondered if it was because she was stoned and hadn't been out of the apartment in weeks. Months. She was acutely aware of the way she'd performed for the elegant hustler on the phone. Brilliant, Rajiv had cooed. I'll send a confirmation letter to your agent.

Don't bother. He's dead.

For once Rajiv seemed at a loss for words. Oh. Sorry.

Nothing to be sorry about. We all have to die at some point, Mr. Rajiv. Am I pronouncing your name correctly? I tend to Frenchify when in doubt, so correct me if I'm fucking up . . . *Rahh-zheev.*

Rajiv's tone was no longer so ingratiating. I'll send the letter directly to you, then. Or would you prefer e-mail?

Right now Eleanor is distressingly sober. If she had her gin, she could pass out for a few blessed hours. Then get up and try to write. She no longer dreams. Or if she does, has no recollection of it. Days after Yvonne died, her dreams were vivid and charged, like the dreams of a young woman. Yet she was bereft. Stunned and bereft. Eleanor felt guilty and ashamed. Told no one about her strange, electric dreams. Not that there was anyone left to tell.

She turns the TV on. Thank God for cable. All those dyke chefs and buff trainers flaunting lurid tattoos and spiky hair, all those short, fat, aspiring supermodels, all those pattern makers, decorators, and *stylists.* Thug wives, porn stars, trannies looking for love. Glorious wonders of the world. She would spend the rest of her solitary life embracing the sordid confessions, elaborate menus, and weepy makeovers of the twenty-first century.

The body's broken down. Eleanor writes slowly in her eighty-nine-cent

Marble Composition notebook, trying not to grip the gel pen so hard. Mimi—who was not an especially thoughtful or generous person—had recently surprised her by bringing over a set of assorted gel pens from Staples. Midnight, Fuchsia Fire, Emerald City, Tomato Royale, Blue Moon. My kid swears by these, Mimi said. They're the best for your fucked-up hand.

Eleanor's right middle finger—the swollen one—is starting to throb more than usual. *Yet keeps breaking down. Life without Y. A purge. Big round holes. Polka dots of memory. The trannies are back, but it makes no difference now. I've closed the door, and the silence is huge.* On the opposite page, Eleanor draws a face covered with eyes. It is less painful to draw than to write. She goes back to writing:

I am old I am lost I am dying. (she is old, she is lost . . . etc.?)
But I (she) still want my (her) cigarettes and gin.
And my hashish and coke.
And though hash makes me/her paranoid
and cocaine does not—
Dear God what rhymes with not?
Clot. Snot. Blot!

Nonsense, Eleanor thinks. Tedious shit nonsense.

For the reading at Volga, she wants to create something startling and fresh. What was it Rajiv had said about Thursdays being a big deal? We've given you the top slot, Eleanor. *Thursday's the new Friday.* Something new would make the journey out of her cave worth the effort. This reading would be her last, she was sure of it. Would Ben and Nneka come to Volga and watch her make a total fool of herself? Eleanor tosses the notebook aside and grabs the remote, on the hunt for a *Law & Order* rerun. Even one of those dumb spin-offs would do. Jerry Orbach's long, horsey face suddenly appears, rendered in dynamic, streak-free, high-definition. *Ta-*

tung! A pale, unhealthy-looking young woman has come to Jerry for help. O joy. She's Jerry's prodigal daughter, a junkie trying to get clean. The episode's a classic, one of Eleanor's all-time favorites. The scene between father and daughter feels a little too sad and too real. Each of Jerry's eyebrows frozen in a skeptical arch. Too much Botox? What season could this be? Had Jerry already been diagnosed with prostate cancer? Eleanor giggles. What a trivia bimbette I've become. Turn off the TV. Go back to writing your tedious shit magnum opus. *Sought. Clot. Blot. Fraught.* Where, oh, where the fuck is Mimi?

The gastric cancer has metastasized to the brain. We've got a couple of options, but— Meyer Griswold was the name of Yvonne's oncologist. He had delivered the news in a calm drone that Eleanor found oddly refreshing. She and Benjy were sitting in the doctor's dreary office at St. Vincent's. Beige, windowless. No trace of the personal, just the requisite framed diplomas and citations hanging on the walls. Eleanor remembers the doctor saying something about the cancers being treatable. Treatable, but incurable. Like the cruel refrain to a song. Or maybe Eleanor misheard on purpose. She remembers turning to look at Benjy. Dank, bitter wind. Gnashing of teeth. Too many lesions and deaths, and now she was numb. She remembers the doctor clearing his throat. Benjy slumped down in his chair, devastated.

Yvonne refused to undergo any more radiation or chemo. *It's killing me faster than the fucking cancer.* Her eyes were clear, and she was still her feisty self when she said this. Whatever you want, Eleanor said. After Dr. Griswold removed the tumor in Yvonne's brain (size of a tennis ball!), Eleanor brought her home. Their old bed was donated to Housing Works, to make way for the rented hospital bed. Wide enough for the two of them, Eleanor had made sure of that. The point being that Yvonne was going to recover and live for a long time. Three of her paintings had been chosen for the Venice Biennale; Yvonne was convinced they were still going. *Have you booked our flights yet? I refuse to stay at the Gritti. Fuck the*

Gritti. Find us something not in San Marco, please. Maybe Benjy can take time off and join us. Tell him the trip's on me. Benjy and you and I in Venice. Won't that be fun?

She did not recover. Mostly Yvonne slept, or floated in a morphine dream. Eleanor would wait until the nurse was out of the room to sit by the bed and speak to Yvonne in a low voice. You'll get a kick out of this, babe. I finally went and did it. Splurged on one of those forty-inch flat-screens, like you were always wanting me to get. DVD player, all that stuff. Had to ask Mimi to help set it up. In fact, she went shopping with me at Best Buy on Twenty-third. They were having a sale. That chick is not intimidated by electronic gadgets! It's good to have a young friend like that, don't you think? I'm such a friggin' Luddite and can't deal with any of it, as you know— Eleanor could not believe the insanity of her monologue. Yvonne's eyes were closed, but her mouth hung open in a faint, mocking smile. Eleanor touched Yvonne's hand. Her skin as transparent and brittle as rice paper. *Can you hear me?* Yvonne hiccupped. The sound somewhere between a cough and a sigh. Then she farted.

It was surprising how long it actually took Yvonne to die. That final year Eleanor could barely keep up with the stream of people in and out of their increasingly chaotic apartment. Delivery guys from the pharmacy and the supermarket. Grace, the private nurse. Benjy, of course. An eerie young woman claiming to be some long-lost, favorite niece of Yvonne's from Chicago crashed on the couch for nearly two weeks until Eleanor finally snapped out of her daze and asked her to leave. Tibor de Lyn of Impure Gallery, Yvonne's longtime dealer, always came on Friday afternoons with his new bride, the luscious and aptly named Plum. She was his fourth wife, a graduate student majoring in atmospheric and planetary science at Columbia. Tibor was one of those short, virile, Old World types, a barrel-chested man of ninety with a shock of white hair. He had made Yvonne a lot of money over the years and probably—Eleanor suspected—skimmed quite a bit from her too. How's our girl doing today? Tibor would ask in his soft, raspy voice. Not too bad, Eleanor might answer. Or: Bad. Or: Dumb question, Tibor.

Sometimes it was all a little too much. I'm going out for some air, Eleanor would announce to Grace. I'll be right back.

No rush, Miss Delacroix. I'm here, the nurse would say.

Eleanor liked walking along the river, past Stuyvesant High to Battery Park. One time she decided to go to a movie. It was around noon on a weekday, and there were too many mediocre choices at the oddly suburban cineplex in Battery Park. She can't remember which movie she chose to watch, but she remembers sitting in the top row of the vast, empty theater, snorting coke and weeping uncontrollably.

Sometimes she'd walk the other way, toward Chelsea Piers. Not as aesthetically pleasing, but what the hell. Even on rainy or unbearably cold days, the meandering strolls usually did her good. The now family-friendly esplanade along the Hudson so pleasant and picturesque. *Hudson River Park.* What irony, Eleanor thought. Though the loud, flashy, and defiant baby dykes and gay boys from the Bronx—pants worn so low past their hips Eleanor marveled at how they could walk—were still cutting school and showing up. One sunny afternoon Eleanor lounged on the Astroturf lawn and watched the preening boys line up to rehearse what looked like fashion-runway poses, angular and imperious. The boys were very serious and kept at it for a long time.

She remembers sitting on the curb of the West Side Highway in shock. Was it only eight years ago? Yvonne was not yet diagnosed, and the scenic esplanade was still under construction. The highway was shut down, except for emergency vehicles and the flatbed trucks carrying twisted airplane parts. She could be remembering it all wrong, of course. Maybe the flatbed trucks and rolling tanks didn't appear until the next day, September 12.

By then the flag-waving patriots would stake their claim on every median, cheering and holding up homemade signs whenever an armored vehicle or fire truck whizzed by.

GOD BLESS AMERICA!!!
SUPPORT OUR TROOPS!!!

The syrupy, toxic stink of burning rubber and plastic made it hard to breathe. The air heavy and hot. Fluttering ash and pieces of paper. Eleanor remembers her neighbors, a solemn and scraggly crowd milling about the deserted highway, everyone too scared to go back to the solitude of their apartments. Comfort in numbers—now, there was a truth. She turned her head and saw a building forty-seven stories high collapse in a swirling mass of black, fiery clouds. It's down! 7 World Trade Center's down! shouted Lester, the Trinidadian longtime super of her building. His voice was cracked and filled with wonder. Coco Schnabel stood with her bulldog, looking stunned and bewildered. Eleanor almost felt sorry for her. Eleanor remembers Yvonne wearing baggy khaki shorts that day, and a faded, 2PAC "All Eyez on Me" T-shirt with the sleeves cut off, one of Benjy's hand-me-downs. Dowdy, paint-splattered Birkenstocks on her feet. Gorgeous, graying, wild-eyed Yvonne, pacing back and forth, trying to get her son on the phone. *My cell's not working. I need to find him.* The procession of ghostly people clutching briefcases marched past them like a dream. Heading uptown, covered in white ash and dust. Their silence eerie. Yvonne gripped Eleanor's arm so hard it hurt. Let's go home, she snarled. I need to use the landline. Reach Benjy. Make sure he's all right.

They heard the old Bakelite rotary phone—which Eleanor had refused to part with—ringing inside their apartment. Yvonne unlocked the door and ran to answer it. Hello? Oh. Just a minute. Disappointed, Yvonne handed Eleanor the receiver.

Yes.

Eleanor Delacroix? A young woman's voice, crisp and professional.

Eleanor held her breath.

Sasha Collins from the *New York Times.* We're asking different writers to contribute response pieces to the—

I went to Westbeth and voted against Giuliani, Eleanor said, interrupting her. There was only one poll worker left and she was scrambling to get out of there, but I insisted on voting anyway. Nuts, right?

It's for the op-ed page, Sasha Collins continued, after a brief pause. We understand you live downtown. Did you actually see—

Nope, Eleanor remembers saying. Not a damn thing.

Yvonne was relentless in her efforts to locate Benjy. Calling his friends and lovers, the few whose numbers she knew. No one had seen or heard from him. Eleanor remembers walking as far as Canal Street with Yvonne but being turned back by the National Guard. Ben was waiting outside when they got home. Yvonne wailing as she threw her arms around him. *Where the hell have you been?* He stayed with them that night. While Benjy and Yvonne slept, Eleanor pulled a hardcover copy of *California Melancholy* from the box that had been delivered just that morning, before anyone knew about the first plane flying into the tower. She stared at the glossy, elegant jacket, the color of pale, golden sand. Her book was doomed, she knew. Now the world had more urgent matters to ponder. Eleanor put the book back into the box and went into her study. She sat down at her computer and typed out a one-page story using the following words: *flashlight, battery, bananas, coffee, child, water, ramen, Cipro.*

Sometimes it was all a little too much. I'm going out for some air, Eleanor would announce to Grace. I'll be right back.

No rush, Miss Delacroix. I'm here, the nurse would say.

At the Chase branch in Sheridan Square, Eleanor would withdraw a significant amount of cash. Then head over to Cleo's apartment on

Bedford to buy more blow to keep herself going. Cleo was recovering from a stroke and about to retire from a lifetime of dealing. I've been a faithful customer, Eleanor whined. How can you do this to me?

Sorry, hon. I'm moving to Staten Island to be with my niece and her kids. My heart's a piece of shit, Cleo said. Look at me—I'm using a walker, for fucksake! The next stroke's gonna leave me completely paralyzed and brain-dead, if I don't quit.

But what am *I* supposed to do?

Cleo gazed at Eleanor in disbelief. What a narcissist you are.

Never said I wasn't.

Cleo laughed in agreement. I can turn you on to some young, enterprising types. This city's full of them. After a pause, she added: They deliver.

Thugs, Eleanor said. Not to be trusted.

Well, then maybe *you* should quit.

Over my dead body, Eleanor snapped.

Eleanor remembers following Cleo into the kitchen. Seeing the depressing pile of unopened bills, Social Security and AARP newsletters stacked on the kitchen table. A tacky brochure from some outfit called Catholic Cemeteries lay on top of the pile. "Complete The Circle Of Life In Harmony With The Church." What the fuck's this? Eleanor asked, picking up the brochure to take a closer look. The hits keep on comin', Cleo said with a shrug. Do what I do, Eleanor said. Toss that shit in the garbage. Cleo waited before asking, How's Yvonne doin'? Not really expecting an answer. Eleanor's face an inscrutable mask of cool. She watched with keen interest as Cleo weighed the mound of white powder on the antique table scale. Funny, Eleanor mused out loud. How you've never needed a gun.

When you were doing business, I don't recall *you* owning a gun, Cleo said. She was smiling when she said this. Her teeth—what was left of them anyway—hung loosely from inflamed, receding gums. Cleo who had once been sexy and bad-boy handsome. The James Dean of Bedford Street.

Sure that's an ounce?

Gimme a fuckin' break. After all these years, why would I burn you?

Eleanor put her money down on the table.

Cleo dipped into the powder with the talon on her pinkie and had herself a little sniff. Just like old times, she cackled, handing the Baggie to Eleanor. Give a kiss and hello to Yvonne for me, will ya?

She's mostly out of it. Asleep.

I understand, Cleo said. You take care now, Eleanor.

Sometimes it was all a little too much. The stash of blow not enough to keep her dry-eyed and detached. She grew paranoid of Grace, wondering if the nurse had taken note of her frequent trips to the bathroom. The apartment—except for the room where Yvonne lay—had grown squalid. A sure sign of her drug-addled incompetence, Eleanor thought. She decided to hire Tibor de Lyn's former housekeeper, a Serbian woman named Mattia, to scour the apartment and help with whatever needed doing. It's going to be a constant battle, Eleanor warned her. My friend is terminally ill. Almost as soon as she said it, Eleanor was disgusted with herself. *Friend*. But was *lover, wife, companion,* or *partner* any better? *Spouse,* domestic like a mouse. Inadequate words. Hollow, despicable.

Mattia's stare was piercing. Mr. Tibor and Miss Plum explain everything.

Anything can compromise her immune system, Eleanor continued. Every room, every surface has to be scrubbed and disinfected. Like a hospital.

The two women sat there for a moment without saying anything.

Can you do it? Eleanor finally asked.

Easy, Mattia said. Also I cook.

She was punctual and wore the same outfit every day. Baggy knockoff jeans, a maroon Old Navy fleece, white sneakers. A gold cross dangled from a chain around her thick neck. Eleanor couldn't bear the constant smell of bleach and disinfectant, but Mattia did her work efficiently and, for a time, kept the germs and wolves at bay.

Benjy liked showing up without calling ahead, a different girlfriend by his side every time. How's my mother today? he'd mumble, brushing rudely past Eleanor. Making a point. Eleanor thinking, Oh how he hates me. *O how he hates me,* she wrote in her notebook. While Benjy sat with his mother, his girlfriend of the moment would wait in the living room. Often for hours. His women tended to be exotic, with names like music and poetry. Francesca, Daphne, Arabella. There was a brazen waif named Jasmine, who Eleanor caught in the act of stealing a small sketch of a pensive man smoking a cigar. The framed sketch hung in the living room, next to the window. If you look closely you'll notice Yvonne did that on a cocktail napkin, Eleanor had said as she approached the surprised young woman. The napkin's from the bar on the terrace of the Hotel Nacional in Havana. Yvonne was waiting for me, and of course I was late. Very late. Have you ever been to Havana?

No, Jasmine whispered, holding the framed piece against her bony chest and starting to back away.

I'm not going to hit you, Eleanor wanted to assure her, but she didn't. Instead she extended her hand. Well, this ridiculous embargo or whatever they call it should end soon. Then maybe Ben can take you to Cuba. Now, may I have the drawing back, and will you please leave my fucking house?

And then Nneka came into Benjy's life. A majestic and luminous presence, adored by all, including Eleanor. The effervescent supermodel had needed only one name. *Nneka.* Which, according to Benjy, in her native Igbo language, meant "supreme mother."

Law & Order ends. Eleanor mutes the infomercial that follows and surveys the mess in the living room. Time for her to downsize and sell the apartment. It was much too big now, too cluttered with memories and lacking in joy. There was a hefty profit to be made, in spite of the current shitty economy. The Far West Village had been transformed into a highly coveted, family-friendly barrio of cupcakes and Labradoodles and faux-Parisian bistros, after all. Eleanor took pride in being a veteran of shitty economies. Nothing like being born in the Year of the Great Crash. She and Yvonne had bought their apartment back when AIDS was rampant and no one wanted to live among the derelicts and the drag queens and the butchers who plied their bloody trade. The owners were desperate and sold at a considerable loss, so there was still money left for Yvonne to purchase the shabby but light-filled loft on East Broadway to use as her painting studio. When Benjy grew old enough, he started crashing there. Benjy who in a drunken rage accused Eleanor of exploiting his mother's fame and stealing her money. Eleanor remembers being so stunned she hadn't even bothered to defend herself. With Yvonne dead, the firetrap in Chinatown is all his. Eleanor smiles to herself. Why not just give the West Village apartment to Benjy and Nneka as a gift? Where she was going next, to live out the last few hours of her life, didn't really matter. If Benjy decided to take the high road and reject her gift, then so be it.

Soon the sunrise, the rumble and hiss of garbage trucks, the raucous banter and shouts of men with their cranes and forklifts. They would drill and bang and grind the day away as their work on the mammoth steel-and-glass condos continued. Eleanor peeks through the blinds, hoping to glimpse Mimi on her way home. The darkness slowly recedes into hazy morning light. She nods off standing up. Nods off thinking, Wicked cunt. I shouldn't have fronted the wicked cunt all that money. The sharp sound of the doorbell jolts Eleanor awake. Through the peephole she sees a shadowy face. Eleanor decides it belongs to Mimi and opens the door. Did you blow all my money, cunt? Oh, jesusfuckingchrist, I'm sorry, Violet.

Violet giggles.

Violet?

Violet takes a deep breath and pulls herself together. She swaggers into the apartment. Can't find my keys. Mind if I wait here for my mom?

Eleanor slides the dead bolt back in place. She does not know the fourteen-year-old well, feels slightly intimidated by her. May I ask who let you into the building?

Violet's eyeliner is smeared. She stinks of cigarettes. I followed some guy in.

Not a wise thing to do. There's been a string of—

I'm here, aren't I? Safe. And . . . *sound.* Violet starts laughing again, stops herself.

It's very late.

Or very early, depending on how you look at it. Violet collapses on the sofa, picks up the remote. A *Project Runway* rerun captures her attention. Heidi Klum in the midst of solemnly dismissing a flamboyantly costumed male contestant. *Auf Wiedersehen.*

Violet turns to Eleanor, her tone baiting. Think she's hot?

Bit too Aryan. Not my type.

She's *hot.* Violet has trouble finding the packet of Drum buried in her large bag. Okay if I smoke?

Go right ahead. But you've got to roll me one, too.

Violet takes forever to roll a cigarette. Why'd you call my mom a cunt?

Sometimes she acts like one. She'd be the first to admit it.

Violet concentrates on rolling another cigarette for herself. The old woman and the young girl light up and smoke in silence. They sit side by side on the sofa, but not too close. The loud, cheesy commercials go on for an eternity. Eleanor glances at the remote in Violet's lap. Could you please mute the damn thing? Violet acts as if she doesn't hear, eyes glued to the TV screen. Punishment, Eleanor thinks. The nerve, Eleanor thinks. Lucky she's just a kid. Finally, blessedly, another episode kicks in. Scissors, needles, swatches, pins, ticking clocks, sleepless nights. Tears and more tears. *Bitte verzeihen Sie mir, Heidi! Auf Wiedersehen.* Violet entranced by it all, dark eyes brighter and bigger than ever, pupils dilated.

What about your mom? Violet suddenly asks, taking Eleanor by surprise.

I beg your pardon?

She's dead, right?

Long ago and far away, Eleanor answers.

Was she a cunt?

It is Eleanor's turn to stare at Violet.

Was she a cunt? Violet repeats.

Poor Ann was much too fragile and oppressed. A product of her generation, as the saying goes.

Ann.

That was my mother's name, yes. Well, actually, it was Ana. Ana Rosario.

Doesn't sound white. I thought you were white.

I'm a woman of mystery.

Word, Violet murmurs. She is trying hard not to be stoned and studies Eleanor with awakening interest. You loved her? Your mom, I mean.

Oh, yes. And hated her, too. While we're on the subject of family, who are your grandparents?

Wha?

Your mother's parents. Do you know them?

They're dead. Long ago and far away, Violet adds, with a loopy smile. The kid's actually quite endearing when she smiles, thinks Eleanor.

Your father's?

They live in Houston, FYI. And they can't stand my parents or me.

Eleanor rolls her eyes. Houston. That's *rich.*

They are, says Violet. Mad rich. And *très, très* weird.

Slave

The woman is wide awake, curled inside a sleeping bag that smells of charred ash and sex. She is small and thin and naked, in the grip of a terrible fever. She glances at the concrete wall just a few feet away from her. She has enough strength left. She could crawl over there and bash her own head against the cinder-block wall. Keep bashing her own head until—

The woman knows that the silence is temporary, that wrathful demons are toying with her, that the man and his wife will be home soon, without the children. They have taken the little innocents somewhere, but she tries not to think about the man and his wife and what they are capable of, and think about death or escape instead. Is escape really possible? It hurts when she moves and when she thinks, but she must try. Try to get on her feet and run—or, if necessary, crawl and make her way up the basement stairs. Summon the strength (Dear God, Dear Albertine, Dear Mama, Dear Frank, Dear Jesus, Dear Blessed Virgin Mary) to break down the locked door that leads to the kitchen where she used to feed the twins. Two overfed, placid innocents who are really still babies, barely walking and too young to understand anything.

The woman slowly turns so she is on her back and tries to sit up, resting on her elbows. Her lungs feel as if they are filled with stones. In spite of her difficulty breathing, she feels an urge to laugh. She coughs a racking, phlegmy cough instead. Sometime ago (was it months? days?) the wife flew down the basement steps, a banshee wielding a flashlight in one hand. The woman in the sleeping bag shut her eyes and froze, expecting the worst. The wife never uttered a word, shining the powerful light on the helpless figure crumpled on the floor. This went on for some time. The wife walked around slowly, bending down to observe her victim closely and from various angles. The woman in the sleeping bag felt the intensity of the light through her eyelids and tried not to move. When the wife grew bored and finally left, the woman in the sleeping bag let go a stream of piss.

The man and his wife took her clothes away when they locked her in the basement. The basement's what you'd imagine—a dank, subterranean wasteland of discarded furniture, file boxes, and broken things.

The woman in the sleeping bag coughs another deep, rumbling cough that seems to emanate from the soles of her feet and makes her shake. The last time the man checked on her (how many months, days, eternities ago?), he announced in a flat tone of voice that she had pneumonia. The woman who has always been a victim surprised herself by daring to speak. *How long before I die?* The man did not respond. He seemed worried, but angry with her, too. As if getting sick were her fault. The man—foreigner, husband, father, doctor—no longer found her desirable and could hardly look at her. When he did, his look was filled with disgust. The wife, on the other hand, visits often and seems more fascinated than ever.

Where have they taken the children? Have they killed them? The naked woman struggles to remember her prayers. *And now I lay me down to sleep. I pray the Lord their poor little souls to keep. Bless me, Father. For I have sinned.*

Agnes has sinned and is a fool, a whore, and a liar. Her own mother embraced her lies, reveled in how well she was doing, and was careful not to pry too deeply about the exact nature of her new job. And all the other jobs before that. Dear blind Mother, who can no longer work and lives in a constant state of emergency. Money, send money, more and more money! The older her mother gets, the more she needs. A new roof, a water buffalo, insulin. Agnes was happy to accommodate her mother and sent her every bit of money she made. Until they stopped paying her, until they took her passport and cell phone away and she was forbidden to leave the house. Every sheet of paper, every pen or pencil was removed. The husband took the computer to his office. Agnes was still living upstairs, in the back room next to the children's bedroom; there was still a semblance of routine as far as the children went. The wife promised that everything would be returned to her, as soon as certain conditions were met. She should've tried to escape back then, while there was still a chance. She should've threatened to kill those children if they didn't let her go. What a fool she was, what a gullible whore. Before she grew weak and sick and even more confused, the husband and his wife sometimes said they loved her. Then they locked her in the basement.

If she breaks down that door and runs outside screaming, the neighbor—what was his name? Rocco something. Sir Mr. Rocco Something would help her. Sir Mr. Rocco was retired and seemed to be the only one in the prosperous, picture-perfect township who was curious about her. Before she was forbidden to go outside, the woman would take the children in their double stroller for walks in the long, boring, quiet afternoons. How ya doin', pretty Agnes? Sir Mr. Rocco would call out. Everything copacetic? The old man would glance at her chest and tell the same old story about going AWOL during the Vietnam War. He had fled to her country. Paradise, he called it. Anything goes. *The heat, the women, the dope, the beer, the sex. Lost my head, got thrown in the brig. My God, Agnes. Gotta say, it was worth it.* The children whined and squirmed in their stroller. The woman tried not to show her unease and listened politely to what Sir Mr. Rocco was saying. He would save her if he could, she was sure of it.

Don't ever talk to that horny old son of a bitch or go near him again, the wife had said about Sir Mr. Rocco. The wife who spoke perfect English, without the slightest trace of an accent. Rocco's undercover DHS! He can have you deported! Which means trouble for us, you understand?

But Sir seems like a nice man.

What? What did you say? The wife slaps the woman, hard. The force of the slap takes the woman by surprise and brings tears to her eyes. She swallows her tears. The wife slaps her again, then again. The wife's eyes are bright and hard. She seems to be enjoying herself.*

* The above is the scenario starring the vanished Agnes as Mimi imagines it. A scenario she would like to share with her brother Carmelo but doesn't. A scenario she would like to share with Eleanor when she finally sees her. The scenario might evolve into her next movie, another gorefest about unwitting young women who find themselves in precarious situations. Maybe Mimi could call it *Homeland Security.* Something ironic. She wonders if Agnes might still be alive. Alive and hiding in the woods, out there somewhere in woodsy, remote, haunted New Jersey. But of course Mimi knows better.

End of the World

It would've been so easy, Eleanor thought, to pick up the phone and ask the fancy liquor store with the clever name—Spirits Something—to deliver an entire case of gin right to her door. Why had she bothered with Mimi? Eleanor, who knew the answer but nevertheless enjoyed beating herself up, then went on to beat herself up even more for allowing Violet—Mimi's daughter, no less—to so rudely invade her apartment. Eleanor's delicious self-flagellation was interrupted by a rather melodramatic burst of lightning and crackle of thunder. Violet, roused from her TV trance, rushed to the picture window and pulled up the blinds. Shrieking gusts of wind followed another deafening explosion of thunder. Then a barrage of hail.

Roll me another smoke, would you, Violet?

Check it out, Violet said, ignoring Eleanor's request. All this stuff's, like, flying around! Are there tornadoes in New York—in the *winter*?

This planet's fucked, dear. I wouldn't be surprised by anything.

Whoa, Violet murmured, enthralled by the furious spectacle swirling just a few feet in front of her. You gotta see this, Eleanor!

Eleanor muted the volume—they were into reruns of *Dog Whisperer* by now—and joined the young girl at the window. She could barely move her neck, and her lower back was throbbing from sitting on her ass all night in front of the goddamn television. Doing nothing, nothing doing. Forgive me for turning into such a cliché, Yvonne. Eleanor tried not to think of the biscuit tin full of dope hidden in her bedroom. Should she try acting like an adult and offer to cook breakfast for the girl? She vaguely recalled an unopened package of bacon and a half dozen eggs in the fridge. A bag of Sumatran coffee beans that had been in the freezer for years. Surely all rotten by now. She used to know her way around a kitchen, used to love cooking for Yvonne and their friends. But in these dreary, tedious days of nothing, food was no longer a pleasure or priority.

Eleanor picked up an old British *Vogue* that lay on the coffee table. With a thick black Sharpie, she scribbled a frantic note to herself across the face of spooky, flame-haired cover girl Karen Elson (a dead ringer for Yvonne in her youth). CREATE MEMORY NOTEBOOK!!! Yes, Eleanor promised herself, I will record a daily account of my purchases and activities in one of my Marble Composition Books. Bacon, eggs, gin, cocaine: bought on such and such a day, month, year. If so, where and from whom? Did I drink enough water, eat any food, leave the apartment at all today? Yesterday? Oxygen. Shelf life. Remember to remember.

Tears streamed from the young girl's eyes. What's wrong, Violet? Eleanor asked. She did not need a teenage drama queen falling apart in front of her.

I don't know, Violet said.

Well, there must be something—

NO.

Eleanor waited before asking the inevitable question. What are you on?

WHAT?

You're high.

NO!

There's no need to lie to me, Violet. Maybe your mother hasn't informed you, but I know about being high.

You mean cuz you're a drunk, Violet sneered.

Among other things. So, Violet dear—what are you on?

Violet clamped her hands over her ears and squeezed her eyes shut. The visions kept coming. Gorillas, dancing tombstones, anonymous naked women with their legs spread, leering, horrible. Leave me alone, you bitch! Violet sobbed.

Eleanor left the furious girl and returned a few moments later with a wad of tissue and a glass of water. Blow your nose and drink some water, Violet. I swear you'll feel better. The young girl glared at Eleanor but did as she was told. Does your father know where you are? Don't you have school today? Eleanor asked in the gentlest and most neutral tone imaginable.

I texted him that I was here, Violet mumbled.

Likely story, Eleanor thought. She let it pass. Other people's children were not her concern. She had tried with Benjamin, helping Yvonne to raise him since he was a boy of nine. And where did that get her? To shit and more shit. Ben was her sworn enemy.

You hungry? Eleanor asked Violet.

I'm tired.

So am I. Unbearably exhausted, actually. Maybe I'll try to get some sleep, Eleanor said.

Mom hardly sleeps.

She's suffering from a twenty-first-century affliction. We all are.

Mom's not a sufferer. She's a tweaker.

Eleanor stifled a laugh. Is that so?

Like, you know where she probably is this very fucking minute? Getting stoned with that asshole Bobby. I texted her when I texted Dashiell, but Mom never—

Isn't that boy supposed to be dead?

Yeah, but who really knows, right? Violet fretting, anxious. I mean, look out the window and see for yourself. Who really knows?

Go in my bedroom and lie down, Violet. Your mother will get here when she gets here.

What about you? Where you gonna—

I'll take the sofa, Eleanor said. Love me some sofa.

Save Me, I'm Drowning

Mimi was five blocks from the subway station when the wind picked up and the hail came down. She considered going back to Carmelo's sad-ass apartment to wait it out, knew it was a bad idea, and kept walking. The thick, punishing rain and ferocious winds made it impossible to see or walk any faster. When her rubber flip-flops fell apart, Mimi tossed them aside and slogged on in her bare feet, hoping she wouldn't end up needing a tetanus shot by the time she got home. If she ever got home. A dark sedan that had seen better days pulled up to the curb. The driver, a shovel-jawed man with a dour face, cracked the window on the passenger side of his front seat. Need taxi?

Mimi hesitated before walking over to the car. Thinking, Undercover cop, serial killer, rapist, maybe all of the above. Thinking, Save me, I'm drowning. The driver waited with infinite patience for her to speak, maintaining his dour expression.

How much to Manhattan?

Where Manhattan?

Meatpacking. You know Horatio? Jane? Little West Twelfth?

I know all, said the driver with a grim chuckle. Fifty.

The words flew out of Mimi's mouth, though she knew better. *Fuck you.*

The driver rolled up the window and began pulling away. Mimi flailed her arms and shouted after him. Thirty-five! I'll give you thirty-five!

He watched Mimi climb into the backseat before delivering the bad news. Sixty up front.

But you said—

You are rude.

Say wha'?

There's always subway, lady. Or maybe swim.

The interior of the car smelled of pine deodorizer and armpits. Mimi surrendered her money, along with what was left of Eleanor's. She needed to get home in one piece, deal with the dying animal who was probably already dead, maybe jump into bed for an hour or two and pull herself together before confronting Eleanor. She was soaked and exhausted and couldn't think straight. Fucked. How had everything gotten so fucked up so quickly? She dug into her bag for her cell phone, hoping it still worked. Maybe Bobby had relented and tried to call. She did not believe that he was dead. There were two text messages—one from Dash, the other from Violet. Mimi erased the message from Dash and read the one from her daughter.

@ Elnrs. 4got keys. TMTH!

TOO MUCH TO HANDLE, indeed. It was six-fifteen in the morning, the world was coming to an end, and Violet was with the last person in the world Mimi wanted to see. Mimi slipped the phone back into her bag and focused on the drops of gray rain beating fast and hard against the window. Time to compose a tale of woe for Picasso. *Would you believe my brother asked to see me last night and I had to go all the way to Queens? Would you believe he's been diagnosed with early-stage Parkinson's and that my dumb-ass cousin Agnes has fucking vanished and has most likely been murdered? When it rains, it pours. Would you fucking believe I got mugged on the train by this skinny poet wielding a box cutter? He took my bag, my leather coat, and—get this—the kid even took my fucking five-dollar Chinatown flip-flops?* No, Eleanor would never believe.

Mimi started nodding off. She blinked several times, trying in vain to stay awake. The driver had turned on the heat, an act of kindness that surprised her. He drove in silence, taking it slow and easy through the rain-slick streets. Mimi felt a surge of relief. Perhaps she was safe after all. She closed her eyes. It took a minute or two before her mouth dropped open and she fell into a dream.

The spindly ten-year-old girl with a crescent-shaped scar on her cheek stands before a door. The door is painted a vivid cobalt blue. The girl who stands before it wears a crisp white nurse's costume, a white nurse's cap made of paper pinned to her thick black hair. On the girl's feet are red patent-leather pumps, with very high heels. The shoes are expensive, painful to wear, narrow and pointy as daggers. The tall, aloof young man with fair skin and blue eyes standing next to her specializes in tantric massage, among other things. Agnes, he commands her. Knock on the door. He is precise, insisting that Agnes knock three times in rapid succession. Three times and no more. There is no response to the loud knocking, only silence. The dream luxuriates in this mysterious silence for quite some time. The young man and Agnes hover by the doorway. *I may look like Agnes, but I'm actually Mimi.* The young man lifts his hand and smacks her across the face. OUCH, she cries, spitting out a bloody tooth. THAT HURTS.

What are you waiting for? Open the door. The young man couldn't care less who she really is. He is not capable of love and not afraid of anything.

My tooth! My beautiful canine tooth! Mimi is a broken record, a dusty overplayed CD.

Fuck your tooth, the young man snarls. Better do as you're told, or I'm calling Homeland Security.

She opens the door. Sir Mr. Romeo? Ready for your kundalini massage?

Tantric, the young man corrects her tersely. The bedroom is dark. He pushes his way past her and flicks on a switch. The dream shimmers with light. Romeo Byron is sprawled naked across the enormous bed. His eyes are wide open and his mouth agape, as if in death he were caught by surprise.

Mimi releases a catlike screech. Sir Mr. Romeo? Mr. Romeo! Are you dead?

But dreams being what they are, the corpse of Romeo Byron comes alive and sits up, speaking calmly and directly to Mimi. Well, lovey, I am. Deader than dead, yet nothing's changed, and I am not so free. My apologies for causing you such grief. Too bad we never got a chance to work together.

Mimi's eyes flew open. They were already in Manhattan, heading toward Fourteenth Street. She wiped the drool from her chin with the back of her hand. How long had she been asleep? Mimi glanced out the window, which was no longer speckled with icy raindrops. It was as if the storm had never happened. She rolled the window down, letting in a frigid breeze. A familiar-looking man was waiting for the light, wearing a black down jacket with the hood up. And shades. He seemed cold, in spite of the jacket. Bobby! Mimi yelled out the window in a shrill, hopeful voice. Bobby! The pale sun was doing its best to burn through the lingering mass of wintry clouds. And there, up ahead, was her street.

Prodigal Daughter

Where is she? Mimi handed Eleanor the pack of cigarettes and the half-empty bottle of Beefeater. Eleanor glanced at Mimi's bare feet, then nodded in the direction of the bedroom. What the hell's *this*? Eleanor referring to the diminished quantity of gin and the half-empty pack of Camel Lights. *Where's my change?* Mimi pretended not to hear and headed for the bedroom. Violet was out cold and snoring softly, on top of the bedcovers. The vintage cowboy boots that she wore year-round were still on her feet. Mimi stared at her sleeping daughter, mesmerized. Mimi had not seen Violet in— Was it really only three months ago?

A bit of exposition: When the prickly unit known as Mimi and Dash broke apart, Dash fled to a one-bedroom in Bushwick. Nubile Cheryl followed soon after. The allure of living in a dicey apartment with a paunchy, middle-aged cynic faded after a few months. Cheryl moved back in with her parents in Riverdale, though she and Dash continued to see each other. Violet chose to live with Dash after Cheryl moved out. Violet hated the situation, hated the claustrophobic bedroom that her father gave up to her, but she knew it was the perfect way to punish her mother. Mimi welcomed Violet dropping in, which Violet did from time to time. To yank her mother's chain. To test her.

Such changes, Mimi thought. Violet had grown beautiful and imposing, her body taking up a lot of room on Eleanor's bed. She carefully pulled off Violet's scruffy boots, not wanting to wake her. Violet was not wearing socks. Mimi recoiled from the pungent stink of her feet.

Eleanor sipped from her tumbler of gin and tonic. They were in the living room, dusty and bright with morning sun. I was ready with all these excuses, Mimi said.

Let's hear it.

I got mugged. The mugger drank most of your liquor.

Then gave you back the bottle? Eleanor's tone was scornful. You expected me to fall for that?

Yeah, well. Sorry I can't be more creative. It's been a long night. You mind if Violet stays for a while? I hate the thought of waking her up.

Eleanor shrugged.

Thanks, Mimi said. I really appreciate—

Your kid was tripping when she got here.

Really.

Acid. Or whatever hallucinogenic's in fashion these days.

Mimi was silent. Thinking, And how much does Dashiell know or care?

Eleanor glanced at the tumbler in her hand, now devoid of gin. A new thought occurred to her. She looked hard at Mimi. Need a bump?

Mimi had to laugh. Conscious of Violet sleeping in the next room, she lowered her voice. Jesusfuckingchrist, Eleanor. You mean you've had product all this time but had me running all over town like a fool? What was the point of alla that?

You underestimate me, which is the one thing I've never liked about you, Eleanor said.

I'll pay you back later today, I swear.

No you won't. Listen, kiddo. Relax. It's only money.

Yeah? Wish I could say that.

When you get to be my age, you can.

Eleanor disappeared into the bedroom where Violet lay snoring and returned moments later with a tin box. She made herself comfortable on the sofa, then took her precious time laying out lines on the marble-topped coffee table. Mimi tried not to show her mounting impatience. This batch is practically uncut, Eleanor said. You won't need much, so watch yourself.

K, Mimi murmured. She was about to explode. Was that guy she saw waiting to cross the West Side Highway really Bobby? Man in black, hiding in plain sight. He had not turned around, had walked briskly across the highway when she screamed his name. *Bobby!* Had to be, Mimi thought. Definitely his style.

Eleanor offered her a little straw made of smoky glass. Mimi listened for sounds of Violet stirring in the bedroom before bending over the coffee table and taking a snort. Eleanor thinking, Mothers and their guilt. The coke made Mimi rear her head in astonishment. She struggled to compose herself.

Had enough? Eleanor asked.

Absolutely, Mimi said. She handed the straw back to Eleanor with a grateful smile. The greed in her eyes burned a little too brightly, Eleanor thought. Or maybe it was grief.

Las Meninas

My last year on earth, I asked Eleanor to throw a party in my honor. Out of the fog and into the starry night, I always say. There's only so much pain, doom, and gloom a dying person can put up with, especially a brat like me. My real birthday had come and gone while I was undergoing another futile round of surgery; it was no secret that I probably wouldn't make it to the next one.

Let's have fun, I murmured. A little soiree. Not too much fuss or too many people.

Eleanor hovering by the bed, trying to understand.

No gifts, I said. I don't want any gifts.

I believe that Eleanor attempted a smile. You comfortable, sweetie? I can have Grace—

Comfortable, the euphemism in palliative care for getting someone high. The nurses and doctors all used it. No one, for some reason, said the word *high* when it came to me. Not even Eleanor. You high, sweetie? I can have Grace pump you with a stronger dose of— (No, not even Eleanor.)

Don't invite Grace, I said. Nurses and birthday parties don't go together. You hear me, Eleanor?

Yup.

And no Tibor and no Plum. Fucking predators. I don't want them here.

Got it.

You look pissed off. Did I piss you off?

Absolutely not, Eleanor said.

A party! Booze, salty canapés, the whole bit. First of all, I couldn't really eat or drink, but that was certainly beside the point. After cocktails we were off to dinner at Las Meninas, one of the few neighborhood places left that has withstood every dining trend, every economic downturn and upturn imaginable. (It is still there, on Washington and Bethune.) The owners, a married couple named Larry and Rocio, live above the restaurant. Larry once asked me to paint a portrait of his beloved Rocio as a surprise for her birthday. Originally from Sevilla, Rocio is an earthy, vibrant woman with big tits and big hips, full of zest. But for some reason, the painting I did of her turned out to be dark and sinister. I remember Larry trying not to look horrified. I won't charge you but I won't change a thing, I said to him. And if Rocio hates the painting, feel free to burn it.

They ended up hanging it in the restaurant's main dining room. O the sexy paella! Rocio has taught her Vietnamese chef, Tommy, how to make a mean paella. Full of the sea, briny and moist, a sight to behold. Tastes like your cunt, Eleanor once whispered to me over a meal. We had gone to Las Meninas to make up after some awful quarrel—over Benjy, over some other woman or man I may or may not have been sleeping with. Anyway, Eleanor was drinking a little too much and trying a little too hard to be clever and shocking. I remember rolling my eyes. Amazing the things you never forget, even when parts of you have been removed, your skull's been cut open, probed by a scalpel, and sewn back again.

It may have been the same day or the next or the next after that. You have to invite Benjamin Wilder, I insisted. Be sure to invite— I was stoned from the morphine drip; I was determined to make a real effort. To impose my will, to enunciate my son's entire name. *Benjamin Wilder.*

I left a message, Eleanor said. For Benjy and Nneka.

Nneka! Oh, yes, Nneka. Glorious Nneka. And Benjy's father. May as well invite him, too.

WHAT.

Sebastian, I said. It'll make Benjy happy.

Sebastian's dead, Eleanor said.

You're lying, I said. I was slipping away, my skull encased in bales of cotton.

Grace walked into the room just then. Grace, I moaned. Grace, how old am I?

And then the drift. The blessed, shallow drift.

Oh to be young and reckless again, fucking whoever and whenever I want! I had not been to any doctors yet when I shouted this at Eleanor, but I could smell the sickness oozing from my pores. Actually, I'm exaggerating a bit. There were no symptoms, no stink oozing out of me. Just a feeling.

It may have been later that same night or the next day or the one after that. I was conscious, swimming in a pool of sand. Benjy won't show up, I fretted. Eleanor didn't seem worried. He'll show up because of you, she said. Your son loves *you.*

He thinks we despise him, I said. For being such a suit.

Don't be silly. Are you comfortable? Eleanor asked. Do you need—

I need, I said. Gimme all you got.

It only took a moment. I bared my teeth and snarled in delight. My eyelids fluttered like feathers.

I wore my Miyake. The 100 percent polyester fabric felt cool and welcome against my skin after such a long absence. The doorbell rang. Eleanor adjusted the hospital bed so I could sit up. Probably Benjy, Eleanor said. I expected Benjy to bring a huge bouquet of exotic and intimidating flowers, like he always did. Bird-of-paradise, ginger, plumeria—all my favorites. Please take off shoes, I heard Mattia say. Then Benjy in that snotty, wounded voice: Put these in a vase, would you? And bring them to my mum's room.

Doctor not allow flowers.

Excuse me?

Not in room. Sorry Mr. Benjamin.

My son never got over the shock of seeing his once sexy, robust, and powerful mother transformed into a bald, shrunken old geezer with a beak for a nose. Poor baby.

Hello, Mum.

Where's Nneka? I asked.

Eleanor left the room. Benjy picked up my limp hand and gave it a kiss.

In the Seychelles, on a shoot. She sends you her love, Benjy said. My poor baby looking dejected, trying his best to keep it together.

Your face. There's something new. What—

A beard, Benjy said.

The doorbell rang again. Louder, more aggressive. Or so it seemed.

I winced and moved my head sideways.

That was the doorbell, Mum.

Hurts, I said.

I heard Mattia bark, *Take off shoes.* Mimi entered the room with Eleanor, brandishing a magnum of champagne. Happy birthday, Yvonne!

How old am I? I asked.

Old enough to drink, Mimi said. She beamed at my son. Wazzup, Ben? Long time no see.

What a fabulous slut. You've got to hand it to her, really. Calls herself a filmmaker. Clad for the occasion in a revealing outfit—a gauzy camisole worn over some sort of low-slung, Gypsy skirt that exposed the sensuous paunch of her tawny belly. I understood why Eleanor was hooked. God is in the details, truly.

You look ravishing! I yelled. I should paint you! Making everyone laugh, even Benjy. Though I was nothing but a bag of bones, my voice—when I could summon it forth—was startling.

Treats laid out on a tray table. Bottles of wine, a platter of cheese and sliced green apples, dainty olive and goat-cheese tarts Eleanor had whipped up with Mattia's help. Mimi popped open the champagne. I let out a yelp.

Sorry, I wasn't thinking, Mimi said.

I grew frantic. *Is Ben here?*

I'm here, Mum.

Stick around, I said. Don't go anywhere.

Eleanor poured me a mix of water and champagne. More water than bubbly, actually. I took a sip and frowned. There was too much going on. Clamor and strained festivities.

Want us to leave? Benjy asked. We don't have to do this.

No way, I said. The party's just started.

At one point Mimi excused herself and went off somewhere to smoke. Where'd she go? I asked Eleanor. She'll be back, Eleanor said. Why don't you ask Mimi out? I asked Benjy. She's hot stuff. Have you forgotten? Nneka and I are engaged to be married, Benjy said, rather primly. Well, that shouldn't stop you, I said. I turned to Eleanor. *What do you think of his beard?*

Dashing, Eleanor said.

At one point Mimi reappeared. At one point I caught Eleanor sneaking off to the bathroom. I may have been out of my mind, but I knew exactly what the old girl was up to. A little snort and sniff from that tiny bindle of coke she always kept in her pocket. She made sure to flush the toilet and turn the faucet on afterward, as if she were washing her hands. Finally she emerged. My Eleanor felt good, finally. On top of the situation, her nerves scoured clean.

The reservation's for six-thirty. Shall we go? Eleanor said.

I grew agitated. Don't forget my hat. We mustn't forget my hat.

Benjy pushed me in my wheelchair down the block to Las Meninas. Eleanor, stoned and in a generous mood, followed behind with Mimi. I, too, was stoned. The air felt strange like my diaper and Miyake pleats felt strange. Eleanor had made sure to put socks on my feet before slipping them into those fleece-lined things. She pulled a wool cap over my head and wrapped me in all sorts of shawls and mohair blankets. I remember that none of it mattered. I felt the cold and whined about it like a child.

Look at you in that enchanting dress! Rocio gushed. So beautiful! She was not a very good liar. They had steeled themselves for our arrival. Larry taking our coats, Rocio fussing over me. She led us to our usual table. My voice was loud and strident. ROCIO, I LOVE ME SOME SEXY BOYS AND NO LONGER THINK OF SUCCESS. That is good, Rocio said. Very, very good. I turned to my son and lowered my voice. Don't worry, Benjy. You're going to be rich. Then I pumped up the volume and said to Eleanor, There's nothing left to prove! We've done it all! Several diners glanced in our direction. Sangria for the table? Rocio asked.

I remember this. Tommy sent over a magnificent black cake of bittersweet chocolate and blood oranges that he had baked especially for me. A single gold candle flickered in the center. Everyone in Las Meninas—Rocio and Larry, the eaters and drinkers, the waiters and busboys, the bartender, even Tommy—joined in singing *Happy Birthday, Yvonne!* I asked Benjy to blow out the candle for me; I didn't have the strength. I could not eat my slice of cake. Rocio and Larry came by to ask if everything was all right. Terrific, I said.

I remember this. Paintings of bloody flowers, paintings of ancient jaguars with clenched fists that covered entire walls in grand museums. Paintings of fried eggs and brains. I said to Benjy that night, Your father was a sexy man. Not a bad artist, actually. And rich. I was lucky, you were lucky. I was on a roll. Eleanor let me sip from her sangria. I said to Mimi, Here's hoping you've had great sex!

Mimi laughed. When it's good, it's very, very good.

I laughed, too. Or rather, I made a series of coughing, wheezing sounds and could not stop. Benjy held a glass of water up to my dry, parched lips so I could drink. I drank like an animal. I swam in lagoons and rivers. The open sea. The din in the restaurant faded to a hush. Or maybe I only imagined the sounds muted, the colors drained. I heard my son say, Time to go. Yes, Eleanor agreed, Yvonne needs her rest. She asked for the check. When the bill came, Benjy and Eleanor tossed their credit cards on the table. Eleanor tried giving Benjy back his card, and so on. Really tiresome. The poor waiter went off to the kitchen to find Rocio. She snatched the bill off the table and glowered at him. No! No! Can't you see? Everything's on the house.

I remember Larry patting my arm, Rocio planting a kiss on each of my sunken, cadaverous cheeks. It took balls, as Eleanor might say. My son was drunk. You happy, Benjy? I asked him. He nodded. *I am, Mum.* Mimi sat there serenely, gazing at us without saying a word. What's going on in that pretty head of yours? I asked her. A movie, she answered. The busboys scurried to clear the plates and glasses and crumbs of paella and cake from our table, the busboys who could not speak English and were sexy and shy and young. They were terrified by my ghastly smile and ravaged face, terrified by the dirty things I kept whispering, dirty things they didn't understand. But they looked at me with kindness and sorrow and love. Knowing, as I did, that the end was near.

The Animal Waits for Her

A few pellets of black shit lay in a puddle of piss. The animal had somehow found the strength to claw its way past the blankets and stale sheets of Mimi's unmade bed, collapsing on the floor with its eyes half closed after emptying its bowels. Mimi stared at the damp, wasted animal. Somehow she found a way to pick it up off the floor and lay it back down on the bed. Thinking, Don't panic. Call Lucy. Lucy Guzmán would walk her through it. The animal did not move or make a sound. Mimi chastised herself for getting high with Eleanor. And with her kid right there, sleeping in the next room. Images sparked and popped in Mimi's overloaded mind. Endless to-do lists recited by myriad voices. The movie. So many loose ends, so many fucking people to call. She felt capable of everything and nothing at all.

She touched it. Patches of fur came off in her hand. *How much longer?* The animal's stench unbearable. A sign. Mimi glanced at the pillow closest to it. Did she have the courage to smother the creature, to end its suffering? No, she did not. Her fingers felt for the tumors rolling around like tiny balls beneath the surface of its skin. The animal twitched at the sharp buzz of the doorbell. Violet calling faintly through the door. *Ma, you there? Let me in.*

Where were you last night? Violet indignant, rumpled, still half asleep.

Nice to see you, too.

I saw you taking pictures at the vigil.

I was *filming,* Mimi said. Trying out this new camera I got.

Yeah? Can I borrow it? Charlie and I wanna make a movie.

Mimi rolled her eyes.

What? Violet said. Think we're retards?

Not you, Mimi said. Maybe Charlie. So if you saw me at the vigil, why didn't you come over and say hey?

Violet shrugged.

It would've been cool to hang out with you, Mimi dared to say.

Violet averted her gaze. Do you think Romeo OD'd on purpose?

We don't know that. It could've been an accident.

Accident. Yeah, right. Where's the beast? Violet suddenly asks.

On my bed. Brace yourself.

Come with me? A pleading look on Violet's face.

The incessant drilling and banging, the shouts of construction workers could be heard through the closed windows. Mimi took Violet by the hand and led her into the bedroom.

Violet gasped when she saw the dark, lifeless shape on the bed. Dull, stubby horns and splintery claws. Who was this shrunken creature? She didn't notice the puddle until she'd stepped in it.

Ewww. My boots!

Take them off and help me clean up this mess, Mimi snapped.

Violet was stunned by Mimi's sudden show of maternal authority. Without a word she took off her boots and set them aside. Mimi left and came back with a mop, a roll of paper towels, and a spray bottle of Clorox. They cleaned up the mess in silence. Violet kept glancing at the bed. Shouldn't we ask the vet to come over or something?

Mimi grunted and kept mopping. When she was done, Mimi sprayed Clorox on the soles of Violet's boots, scrubbing them with paper towels before handing the boots back to Violet. Violet slipped them on and lay across the bed, curling her body around the animal. O Beasty, she crooned. Great, terrible Beasty. She scratched gently behind its ear. The animal's eyes flickered open at her touch. Then closed. Violet buried her face in its wet, ratty fur.

DON'T, Mimi said. You could catch whatever it has.

Not true.

How about this, then? Eleanor said you were high on acid last night. True?

Eleanor's sketchy. How can you trust her?

You still high?

Violet didn't respond.

Why didn't you take the animal with you when you moved to Brooklyn?

Who cares? Violet said. Who cares about anything?

I ran into this kid panhandling in the subway, Mimi said. Wearing one of those hoodies. Thought she was you.

Give her any money?

Yup.

That's good, Violet said.

Her lower lip was trembling and she was about to cry, Mimi knew. Thinking, I'm a shitty mother and this is going nowhere fast. Out loud, Mimi put forth the inevitable question. Does your father know you're here?

Eleanor already asked me *that.*

Were you on acid, Violet? Or should I give up asking and just smack you?

Eleanor's a *beyotch.* Wrong about everything. I ate a bunch of mushrooms, FYI. Violet beamed with pride. This guy I know? He, like . . . brought a bunch back from Mexico!

You're fourteen years old. Is this smuggler some *friend* of yours? Mimi waited. Leave that fucking animal alone and look at me, Violet!

Violet glared at her mother.

You gonna talk to me or what?

He's Dashiell's friend, Violet said. She'd begun calling her father by his first name ever since the split-up.

And this "friend" gave you mushrooms? Does your father know?

Violet kept stroking the animal. I was snooping around. Found Dashiell's stash. Took the mushrooms. And some weed, too. It's really strong. From the same guy, I think. You want some?

I don't like weed, Mimi said. *Snooping around.* You do that a lot? Mimi's mind racing. Should she call Dash and tell him? Mimi felt a twinge of vengeful glee. Fought hard not to show it.

Dashiell's not very good at hiding things, Violet said. Then added, with a smirk, You should know that.

Violet was no doubt referring to a series of steamy online chats between Dash and her former baby-sitter, Cheryl, which Mimi had stumbled upon by accident one night. He'd passed out from gorging on pasta, wine, and weed and forgotten to sign out. And there were no fucking accidents in the fucking glorious universe, as Eleanor had recently reminded her. Only destiny, and Mimi should have known. Dash had wanted to be busted all along.

Out loud Mimi said, You really should respect your father's—

Can I live here with you? Violet asked.

Mimi stared at her, not sure of what she had just heard. How to process.

I can sleep on the couch. Or in your bed, with you.

We'll work it out, Mimi said.

Or maybe you don't want me around. Is it because of Bobby?

Fuck Bobby. Bobby's gone.

Dashiell says he's probably dead. Violet staring back at Mimi intently. Says it's probably your fault.

Really. Your father had the fucking gall to say that?

The animal's sudden, loud cry startled them both. What do we do? What do we do? Violet kept shrieking, Bobby forgotten for the moment. Mimi grabbed her cell and punched in Eleanor's number. The phone rang and rang. Hello? Eleanor finally picked up, sounding surprised.

Can you please, please get over here? Mimi begged.

The phone went dead, and in a few seconds the old woman was at the door. The animal was panting now. Violet grew more frantic. What do we do? Eleanor? Ma? What do we do?

Get something to wrap it in, Eleanor said, her voice calm.

Mimi ran to the linen closet and found Violet's baby blanket, the one Violet had asked her to never give away. The blanket was pale blue and yellow, made of fleece. She wrapped it snugly around the animal's body, holding the animal close to her.

Make sure it's comfortable, Eleanor said. That's all we can do.

Violet stood with her mouth agape as the animal gave a last guttural howl and clawed wildly at Mimi's arm. Then it was over. Mimi's right arm was torn open, bright with blood. Violet fled from the room and locked herself in the bathroom.

Now what? Mimi held on to the dead animal.

Have it cremated, Eleanor said. Keep the ashes in an urn and make an altar. Very Frida Kahlo.

I'm sick of Frida Kahlo, Mimi said. Aren't you sick of her?

Well, if this building had a backyard, you could bury the animal under a tree. Get a little tombstone made. That would be very Ernest Hemingway. But we don't have backyards. Or trees.

Feel like shit, Mimi said.

Yeah. I bet you do.

I have to find money. Or my movie's—

Fucked? The old woman's tone was sympathetic. There are worse things.

I'm fucked.

May I suggest you go deal with your daughter? The rest will follow.

That's very Zen of you, Mimi said. After a pause, she said, I need to get going, or I'm gonna fall asleep standing here.

You'd better disinfect that arm, Eleanor said. I'm heading back to my apartment, but—the old woman hesitated, then lowered her voice—if you need another bump to get through this most unbearable of days, call me.

After Eleanor left, Mimi leaned against the bathroom door and listened to the ragged sounds of Violet's weeping. Mimi was astonished by the violence of her daughter's grief. Violet, Mimi said in a loud voice. Violet, I am here for you.

Fuck you. Fuck alla you!

Fair enough, Mimi said. A moment, then, Intend to go to school today?

NO.

Want me to ask your father to come get you?

NO.

Gonna unlock this door and come out?

NO.

I'm taking the animal to the vet. Wanna come?

Silence from Violet. Followed by a quiet, *No.*

Fine, Mimi said. I understand.

After more silence, Violet asked, What's the vet gonna do?

Make arrangements to have it cremated, probably.

Then what?

I don't know.

Ma, Violet said.

Yes.

I'm hungry.

I'll get stuff. Make you breakfast. Don't go anywhere. Promise?

Silence.

Violet?

I said OKAY! Violet shouted.

Mimi returned to her bedroom and studied the dead animal on the bed. Its head was sticking out of the blanket. She covered its face. Now it was simply a bundle, which she placed inside a large duffel bag. Her arm was really starting to bother her. There were no bandages around, so Mimi wrapped the torn flesh with an old chiffon scarf before putting on a jacket. She did not need strangers on the street looking at her arm or asking questions. She grabbed the bag and said good-bye to Violet through the bathroom door before leaving the apartment. Mimi pressed the "down" button and waited for the elevator. Coco Schnabel emerged, dragging Churchill, her oppressed, drooling bulldog, on a leash. Coming to the next board meeting, I hope? Coco said by way of greeting. Mimi stiffened. Through no vote of Mimi's or Eleanor's, Coco Schnabel had recently been elected the co-op's board president.

I'm kinda swamped. Plus, I don't own, Mimi said. I rent.

That's no excuse. We're planning extensive renovations and need a vote from the shareholders *and* tenants.

When's the meeting?

Thursday at six.

Sorry.

You can't keep being absent and then complain.

I don't complain.

People don't show up, don't participate. Then as soon as the building's repainted, they suddenly have *opinions.* Did you sign the petition? Your pal Eleanor did. We don't need another boutique hotel in the Village. We need—

I'll sign.

Thatta girl. How's the next movie coming along? Didn't see your first, but Eleanor told me about it. Says it's pretty gory. What's it called again?

Blood Wedding.

Got no stomach for gore, Coco Schnabel said.

The next one's gonna be worse.

Mimi made sure to smile. Coco Schnabel had viewed her with suspicion and disdain since the day Mimi moved into the building. Mimi had no idea why, and except for the fact that the busybody could make her life even more miserable than it already was, Mimi couldn't care less. Coco Schnabel smiled back at her. OH, AND BY THE WAY. You didn't happen to see who took my stuff out of the recycling bin, did you? Whoever did it left a big mess, which of course Lester had to clean up. Poor guy. I gave him a nice tip.

Really? Mimi said, feigning concern.

Yes, dear. *Really.* Coco Schnabel yanked at Churchill's leash and waddled off to her apartment. The elevator, which had come and gone over the course of their conversation, looked to be held hostage in the basement. Mimi took the stairs.

Dazed, she walked the thirteen blocks to Good Shepherd-in-Chelsea Animal Rescue. She wondered how she would pay for the cremation. Her AmEx was maxed out. Thanks to her recent Flip video purchase, only $456 was left in her checking account. The duffel bag banged against her leg. A stylish young man approached from the opposite direction, blabbing into an earphone while pushing a cherubic baby in a stroller. Mimi stepped aside to let them go by. Her arm was growing stiff, and she felt like passing out.

At the clinic the new and very young receptionist took note of the distraught, disheveled woman and steeled herself. May I help you?

Is Lucy in today?

I'm afraid I—

Dr. Guzmán. Lucy Guzmán? She took care of my animal.

Dr. Guzmán's not on duty today, but I can certainly—

Mimi dumped the bag on the counter. The animal's inside.

The receptionist's eyes grew wide. Oh-kay.

I want it cremated. The ashes given back to me, said Mimi.

Please have a seat while I call one of our doctors, the receptionist said, picking up the phone. Mimi took the bag and sat in the waiting area. A man wearing green scrubs appeared a few minutes later. His eyes took in the woman nodding off in the chair.

Miss—ma'am? he said, gently touching her shoulder. Mimi jumped at his touch. I am Dr. Vukocevic.

Shit. Was I asleep?

What can I do for you? Dr. Vukocevic asked. Mimi took note of his formality, the hint of accent. He looked almost as tired as she was.

She patted the bag on her lap. The animal died before I could— She was determined not to break down in front of this man. Anyway. Dr. uh . . .

Vukocevic.

Yes thank you ANYWAY Dr. Vukocevic, it happened early this morning, and I didn't know what else to do, so I ran right over here and—

Slow down, Vukocevic said. Please.

Mimi followed Vukocevic into the overheated examination room. She lay the bag on the gleaming aluminum table and slowly took off her jacket, trying not to wince. Vukocevic removed the bundle from the bag and peeled back the fleece blanket. The animal's eyes were glassy and huge.

But they were *closed,* Mimi said.

Happens, Vukocevic said. He passed his hand over the animal's eyes, closing them. Your arm needs attention.

How much is the cremation gonna cost me?

About one hundred and sixty dollars. The procedure is done upstate. You have to sign some forms. We'll have the ashes for you in about a week. Vukocevic gently lifted Mimi's arm and took a closer look at the jagged wounds. He glanced up at her drawn, tired face. Perhaps you want to sit with the body and make up your mind. I can come back when you are ready.

I'm ready, Mimi said. Let's do it. She started to leave but was stopped by Vukocevic. What the hell?

I must clean those wounds.

Excuse me?

No extra charge. Vukocevic squirted a gauze pad with an antiseptic solution and began swabbing Mimi's arm. She turned her head away. You're a kind man, she said.

And funny, too, Vukocevic said.

A lot of death going around, Mimi said after a pause. You heard about Romeo Byron?

Vukocevic looked lost for a moment. The actor?

Yeah. The actor.

I'm sorry. He was your friend?

Mimi grimaced. Friend? Hell no. Then she added, I wish.

Visitation

W*ords, Eleanor. Words strung like a noose around your neck. Words like love and shit and desire. Words like fire and green dress. She asked to be cremated wearing her—*

Eleanor put the notebook away and shook out her hands to get the blood flowing and the throbbing to ease. She hated having to use the laptop, felt no visceral connection to text on a screen, had owned several computers over the years despite her misgivings, and still it made no difference. Try thinking of it as another kind of notebook, Moss, her late agent, had once said. Convenience and speed. A genius bit of technology.

The joints in her fingers were worn to the bone, her bones infested with ganglion cysts, her bones on the verge of cracking, herself on the verge of cracking, how excruciating to write in longhand in her lined schoolgirl notebook. Don't think about it too much, Eleanor. Arthritis, language, and death. That's all it came down to now. The problem with outliving your agent, your friends, your enemies and lovers, with outliving your one and only Yvonne. Perhaps it was time to cancel that Volga gig and kill herself. She had no more to say to the young people or to herself. Eleanor and Yvonne had always agreed on one thing: suicide as an honorable option.

She clicked on Safari and perused the tabloid headlines. A man sues Oprah for $180 million. A woman hog-ties her Yorkshire terrier, then burns him over a stove. No new tidbits about Romeo Byron. No more online speculation regarding his death. Well, Eleanor thought. *That was quick.*

She considered browsing Skanky Panky, the lesbian porn site Mimi had mentioned during one of their getting-high moments. It was right after Yvonne died, and Mimi was talking a mile a minute, snorting up a storm. Gotta warn you, Eleanor. Pretty nasty stuff. Plus, they only show enough. Just enough.

Eleanor snorting up a storm as well, excited and grateful for the younger woman's company, laying out more lines just to get Mimi to stay longer. *Then what?*

Then I dunno. I guess you max out your credit cards, stop paying your mortgage, ruin your life.

Are the girls hot? asked Eleanor.

Mimi lowered her face over the fat white lines. They're skanks.

Skank. Eleanor loved the sound of it. But maybe gawking at wild young things in her present state of mind would depress her even more. The top joint of her gnarly middle finger hurt more than usual. Eleanor glanced at the tin box next to the laptop. Sighing, she pushed it away.

WHERE'S MY HAT? MY FENTANYL PATCH?

Eleanor swiveled around in her chair. Yvonne was huddled by the bookcase. Naturally she had on her signature dress, a pleated lettuce-green concoction by Issey Miyake that had become too big and billowy for her wispy, cancer-stricken self. Yvonne used to wear it to all her openings. Eleanor, in accordance with Yvonne's final wishes, had her cremated in it.

Yvonne rubbed her scarred, bald head. What's all that fucking noise? My brain's going to implode!

Construction. Condo lofts where the printing press used to be,

Eleanor said, trying to stay calm. The High Line. Which might be fabulous when it's finished, but who knows? It's obscene, what these—

Get Benjy on the phone! I'll buy him a condo. It'll be swell, having him for a neighbor, don't you think? I wouldn't mind if you became lovers. You can't go on like this, Eleanor. God forgives you, if there is a God, and I still don't know, ha-ha!

Benjy's dead, Eleanor said. A vicious lie to test the ghost in the room. An aneurysm, sweetie. It was quick.

Lucky boy! Beautiful boy! All death should be quick! Yvonne came closer. Eleanor could smell her hot, garlicky breath. *What about Nneka? How's Nneka?*

In mourning, Eleanor answered.

Yvonne contemplated the huge, dark painting that hung above Eleanor's desk. A blurry figure crouched in a pit, what looked to be a naked woman with the head of a jaguar. Mouth open in a howl. Did Benjy scatter my ashes like he was supposed to? She suddenly asked, taking Eleanor by surprise.

Of course he did, Eleanor answered.

Yvonne kept staring at her painting.

Take that down. Yvonne's voice was cold and commanding.

Now, why would I do that?

It's a piece of shit.

I happen to like it, said Eleanor. It comforts me in your absence.

I have never been a source of comfort to you or anyone else.

Let's change the fucking subject, okay, Yvonne? Would you believe a five-star hotel next to the condos? The same developers. Our dry cleaners—Hector's bodega—all going out of business. St. Vincent's. No more St. Vincent's. We've started a petition to stop them from closing the hospital down, but who knows if we'll win?

You won't, Yvonne said.

I miss you, Eleanor said.

Yvonne began flitting around the study in her voluminous green frock, pulling books and random objects off the shelves. MY HAT. I NEED MY HAT. She tipped over a bowl made of black clay. It fell off the shelf and shattered into pieces. Yvonne plucked a shard off the floor and pointed it at her heart. YOU'LL FIND OUT SOON ENOUGH, ELEANOR. BEING DEAD IS THE SAME AS BEING ALIVE. A MYSTERY.

Gone Missing

Which was too tidy and perfect and not what she really said. Yvonne also called herself God and loudly absolved Eleanor of Felix's death. *You didn't take a hammer and bash his skull in! Ángel did! You weren't even there!* Again, too many exclamation points. Too tidy and perfect. Moss used to warn her against using the declarative. A phone rang and rang from somewhere far away. Eleanor woke in a foul mood, disoriented. She had fallen asleep with her head on a desk—but whose desk? Whose dark, windowless room? Where the hell was she? Her tongue was swollen and tasted of swamp. Disgusting, Eleanor thought. Really disgusting. She took in the destruction around her. Books and papers, jagged bits of clay everywhere. *Are these my things?* Eleanor turned on the desk lamp. The painting was gone.

The phone was ringing. She stumbled out into the sunny living room, tin box in hand, to answer it. She had a feeling. What do you want, Rajiv?

Sorry to bother you, the silken voice said. I would've left a message, but your voice mail didn't kick in.

With her free hand, Eleanor pried open the tin box. She removed a tiny Baggie of cocaine and held it up to the light, not pleased. Bad product. Sticky, congealed into clumps.

Eleanor? Rajiv, anxious. You there?

Yup, Eleanor said. She reached for an ashtray—one of those big, kitschy fifties ashtrays, shaped like a kidney—and pressed it down on the Baggie as hard as she could.

I've got great news, Rajiv said.

Eleanor was too impatient to lay it all out nice and pretty. Too impatient to use the glass straw. One of the house keys would do just fine, she decided, dipping into the Baggie. The first hit was searing, exactly what she needed. Eleanor grunted with pleasure. She forgot about Rajiv listening intently on the other end of the phone. Forgot about the stabbing pain in the joints of her fingers.

Fantastic news, Rajiv continued to gush. Sasha Collins from the *Times*—well, actually, she's also an associate editor for the *Volga Review* and—

Busy girl, Eleanor murmured. Thinking, What fun. She dipped into the powder again, brought the key up to her other nostril and inhaled. By the way, what time is it?

Two-fifteen P.M. Did I *wake* you? Rajiv sounding amused, conspiratorial.

As a matter of fact, you did.

Sorry about that. Really I am. After a pause, Rajiv said, Sasha's way cool.

Eleanor didn't respond.

She's a fan, Eleanor. You've got a lot of fans.

Eleanor lit a cigarette.

Sasha's coming on Thursday and she—

Which reminds me, Eleanor said. About Thursday—

She wants to interview you. That's why I called. Wanted to run it by you first.

I can't do Thursday.

Oh?

I've come down with a terrible case of bronchitis. Eleanor coughed for dramatic effect.

You're not— Am I hearing this correctly? Not showing up? I mean, I'm sorry you're sick, but—

Eleanor heard the anxiety in Rajiv's voice. That's right, she said, enjoying herself immensely. According to my doctor, these bronchial things are highly infectious. Lethal at my age. And what with the swine flu and—

Rajiv quietly hung up on Eleanor. She was delighted by his impertinence. Her respect for Rajiv—nonexistent until that moment—grew. She knew he would call again, offering profuse apologies. If not today, then tomorrow. Eleanor not showing up at Volga meant Rajiv losing face. The young man was never going to let that happen.

Back in her study, eager to start again. Careful to avoid the sharp, broken things on the floor. Eleanor told herself that Yvonne's painting wasn't gone but misplaced. Hidden under the bed, or in the back of a closet somewhere. Yvonne's restless, contentious ghost did not pay her a visit, steal the painting, or make a mess of Eleanor's study. If Eleanor looked hard enough, she would find the beloved painting sooner or later. Stop getting high, she said to herself. Give the tired old brain and heart a little respite. Liver, too.

Eleanor sat down before the computer. Clicked on "New Blank Document." She would look for the missing painting later tonight. Maybe with Mimi and Violet's help. Yes, Eleanor thought. What an excellent idea! Do a little writing, wash your face, brush your teeth, soak in the tub, change your clothes. Eleanor had never been seriously invested in fashion in the same way that Yvonne had been when she was alive, but Eleanor was vain. Though in the last year, Eleanor couldn't think of a good reason to get out of her tattered robe and baggy pajamas. Today suddenly seemed different. Today she was determined to crawl out of her cave and clean herself up, put on lovely clothes (so many of them waiting in the closet), shop for groceries, invite Mimi and Violet over, and cook the three of them a fabulous dinner. Prawn curry with lemongrass, chili peppers, and coconut milk. Saffron rice. A bottle of tart white rioja (or two) to go with everything. Her first stop would be Souk, the spice shop on Bleecker. It had been there since the seventies. A bit of a journey, a bit of a hassle, the hippie proprietor a paranoid bitch, piercing kohl-rimmed eyes on the constant lookout for shoplifters. (Was Souk still in business? Was that paranoid bitch still alive?) But having *real* lemongrass and the right kind of fiery peppers—wicked, tiny, and red—would be worth the effort. If she were ten years younger, she'd walk to Chinatown. To that corner stall on Bayard, near Yvonne's old studio, the corner stall that offered the most fragrant and exotic of ingredients at less than half the price—Eleanor swore—of any market in all the five boroughs. She could probably get her prawns there, too. But Eleanor could no longer move with joy and ease and abandon through those teeming, crowded streets. She was old. Whatever she found on Bleecker Street would just have to do.

Love

Mimi was five blocks ahead, walking south on Ninth Avenue, by the time Aleksandar Vukocevic caught up with her. Out of breath, still in his scrubs, nervous.

May I see you again? Vukocevic asked.

Mimi stared at him, surprised. Her right arm was stinging, dressed and bandaged by Vukocevic only moments ago. Sorry, she said. I've run out of animals.

His dark eyes were full of woe. We can go for a wine. Maybe to the cinema. Whatever you prefer.

A sensitive romantic, Mimi thought. Reckless enough to pursue her down the street. She liked the idea of men being reckless and often mistook it for passion. She suspected that soulful, reckless Vukocevic could be fun—*intense* was probably the better word—in bed. A day ago she would have happily surrendered to the heat of the moment.

I have offended you?

No, Mimi said. Not at all.

Ah, Vukocevic said, relieved. No maybe means yes?

Listen, Doctor. You're hot, but I don't think so.

Alex, he said. Please call me Alex.

Whatever. Mimi quickened her pace.

In spite of her rudeness, he continued walking beside her. How about we try? We have a wine, we talk. If we don't like each other, we say very nice, thank you, Alex, thank you, Mimi, good-bye!

Mimi laughed. You can look up my number when you get back to the animal clinic. You're new there, aren't you?

Only yesterday I started.

And by the way, I smoke cigars. You like cigars?

Vukocevic gave a little shrug. I don't know, but why not? Sure.

So maybe I'll take you to my favorite cigar bar. Maybe.

She turned to go, but he leaned in and kissed her on the mouth, again taking her by surprise. He then walked away. Up close he had smelled faintly of tar and sweat; his kiss tasted of nothing. *Damn,* Mimi muttered to herself, wiping a hand slowly across her mouth. What balls.

She liked to brag about being an orphan, brag that she has never been in love. She admitted to desire, to lusting after elusive men like Dashiell and Bobby. It was all about the self, Mimi would say, when it came to those two. Their masculine beauty, what they could do for her, was what mattered. Mimi understood the exploitation to be mutual. Tit for tat, rule of karma, goes aroun' comes aroun', et cetera. Mimi rolled with the punches. Unlike her brother, Carmelo, she wasn't a sap. Her world was a hostile, brutal place, a brothel to be navigated with exquisite care. Fuck that love shit. Aleksandar Vukocevic, healer and protector of the animal kingdom, would have provided a pleasant distraction. Nothing more.

The old writer, during another of their truth-telling, getting-high moments, had said, I don't buy that you're heartless. I just don't buy it. You love Violet. More than you think.

Because I somehow can't help it? I'm her mother?

Your dishonesty bores me. If I say that your love comes from some dark, twisted place, would that make you feel better?

I don't want to bore you, Eleanor.

Then stop.

She would kill and die for Violet, sure. Wipe Violet's ass, cradle Violet in her arms like she had watched Eleanor cradle a dying Yvonne to the bitter end. She remembers a movie Dashiell rented one night when they were still together. He came home late, in one of his moods. Mimi suspected he was fucking someone (Paula? Cheryl?) or about to be fired. Either way, Dash was snarky, self-righteous. Pissed off about something but not saying what. Going on instead about the movie he'd rented, insisting that she stay up to watch it with him. Violet was in bed, thankfully asleep. Dash drank a lot of wine with dinner (Chinese takeout, too much MSG and cornstarch, but convenient). Mimi wasn't much of a drinker yet, so Dash put away two bottles of moderately priced Chilean red all by himself. She pretended not to notice, poking at the food with her chopsticks while he drank. Violet was three or four then, hyper and funny, relentless in her demands. Mimi was looking for a job, always tired, sick of their lives. A letter accepting her into the Sundance Screenwriters Lab had arrived in the mail that afternoon. The letter should have elated her but didn't.

Without telling anyone and almost as a goof, Mimi had submitted the latest draft of *Blood Wedding* to the Sundance *Directors* Lab. The Screenwriters Lab was of no interest to her. As far as she was concerned, her script was locked and ready to shoot. All she needed was money, plus a producer, or two, or three. But now she was being told that she needed to jump through a few hoops first, and this particular hoop seemed like a waste of time. The thought of her perfect script being torn apart and analyzed by a bunch of so-called experts over the course of five days in Utah made Mimi queasy. *Utah.* A place Mimi had never been. She liked the forceful sound of it. Mimi reread the letter more carefully a second time. The list of screenwriter mentors was diverse and impressive. It seemed as if writers of every kind of movie imaginable—action-adventure, edgy-artsy indie, whatever—had volunteered to come to Sundance to impart their wisdom. Even the old guy who wrote *Rebel Without a Cause.* Mimi was amazed he was still alive and kicking. She had to admit, the invitation was tempting. Round-trip travel, fancy lodging, yummy meals provided three times a day. A working holiday, but a much-needed holiday nonetheless, from Dash and Violet. Thank you, Robert Redford. But no.

The movie Dash brought home was *Sophie's Choice.* Meryl Streep in the role of the Polish woman forced into making a terrible choice involving her two small children. Her helpless, innocent babies. Mimi did not want to watch it; Mimi wanted to throw the unappetizing leftovers in the garbage and go for a solitary walk. She had been indoors all day with relentless, demanding Violet, and now that grim, tight-lipped Dashiell was finally home, she wanted to flee. He was so unhappy, and she could not help him. She waited for the right moment to bring up Sundance with Dash, but the moment looked like it would never come.

This movie's fucking amazing, Dashiell said, inserting the DVD into their brand-new player. Gonna break your fucking heart.

I can't stand Meryl Streep, Mimi said.

He ignored her childish remark, too disgusted to respond. Fuck her. He would watch the movie by himself if he had to, pass out on the sofa with his mouth open like he often did. It beat getting into bed with her, beat lying beside her acting like everything was fine, was cool. Mimi would eventually come around like she always did. She'd sit beside him on the sofa in that grudging way of hers, watch the fucking amazing movie with a skeptical frown on her face. Arms crossed, feet up on the coffee table, smug. SHOW ME WHY THIS SHIT IS SO GREAT, DASHIELL. SHOW ME. Mimi was once the beauty, the wicked fun and love of his life. How did she turn into such a shrew? He actually knew the answer to that one but hadn't bargained on everything going sour so fast.

The diminutive and twinkly-eyed Dr. Nimboonchaj, since passed away from her own ugly battles with cervical cancer, had called Mimi personally with the news. Mimi sensed the gracious doctor wanting to say, Congratulations. Thankfully, she didn't.

Is it too late for an abortion? Mimi asked after a moment of silence. She had never been interested in being pregnant or being a mother. She took all the necessary precautions, insisted men wear rubbers, et cetera, et cetera. *How the fuck did this happen?* Dashiell's last bit of coke, which she was in the midst of sniffing when the phone rang, slowly trickled down the back of her throat.

I can refer you to a colleague, Dr. Nimboonchaj said.

How did this happen? I'm always careful.

Dr. Nimboonchaj sighed. What is it you people say? Takes two to tango. Perhaps your husband—

I've told you a million times. I don't have a husband, Mimi said.

Should I have this baby? Mimi asked Dashiell later that evening. Musing aloud, the question not intended for him at all.

Only if it's mine, Dash said with a charming, arrogant grin.

In spite of her dour mood, Mimi burst out laughing. They kissed.

She could tell that he was stunned, but also pleased by the news of her pregnancy. Aroused, even. I love you, he had said from across the kitchen table. The table not really a table, but a wooden plank placed over the old-fashioned, claw-foot bathtub that took up most of his tenement kitchen. It was where they ate, got high, washed dishes, and bathed. Quaint and maybe sexy, but also a drag. Dash was waiting for her to respond. Was she supposed to say I love you, too? Neither of them would ever find peace, but maybe it was true. This was love, staring her in the face. And now the baby, clearly a sign.

Let's find a bigger place, Dash said. Move in together. Get married.

I don't want to marry, Mimi said. Ever.

All right. But we can live together and have a family.

This is insane, Mimi said. You're insane. We have no money.

There's a job opening at the Lumière Foundation.

Really.

The director of their film/video arts program just quit. It's a decent gig. Benefits, all that shit. Which means I can lie that we're married and get you health insurance.

What about the short you've been working on?

It can wait, Dash said. This is more important.

Which touched Mimi, though she couldn't help but ask, Did you hear about the job through Paula?

Dash shrugged.

Maybe I should apply, Mimi said. I mean, why not compete for the same job?

Another grin and noncommittal shrug from Dash. Mimi lit a cigarette. Dash leaned over and snatched it from her hand. You're a mommy now, he said. Mimi watched him take a drag and exhale before putting it out. Without missing a beat, she lit another one and held it away from his reach. So. You gonna have to fuck Paula as part of the interview?

Dash applied for the job, was interviewed by Paula and a committee made up of Lumière Foundation trustees, was interviewed a second time and, weeks later, finally hired. He did his job with panache; he actually seemed to be thriving. Dash was good at chatting up the stingy donors and patrons, good at flattering and appeasing, at squeezing money out of them. The Lumière Foundation was its own world, and his staff of young, mostly female, over-educated program assistants saw their jobs as temporary and assumed that any day now, they would be recognized as the innovative choreographers, groundbreaking novelists, and electrifying actors they had always thought themselves to be. They were astonished when they found themselves working at the Lumière Foundation two, three, maybe five years later. Just as Dash was astonished that he was still there.

He no longer made his strange, gorgeous films, the short films Mimi loved—all of them in black and white (he had no use for color), all of them thirteen minutes long. He no longer roamed the streets, taking black-and-white photographs of random buildings and random people with his Speed Graphic camera (4x5, like his idol Weegee's camera). Dash was unhappy and—though he jogged in Central Park at least four times a week—putting on weight and drinking too much. And yet they stayed together another seven years.

And their kid, their skittish, brilliant kid, sleeping in her room, peaceful, oblivious. Or maybe not. Their kid was neither blind nor stupid. *She was fucking amazing.* Fucking amazing, his love for her.

A mystery.

Sophie's Choice. It was the beginning of the end. Mimi hovered by the doorway, arms crossed, waiting for Dash to notice her. Okay, why not? Put up with his fucking amazing movie. Whatever he wants. It was the beginning of the end, she knew it was over, why were they still together, why won't I leave, why won't he?

I got this letter, Mimi said. From the Sundance people.

What Sundance people?

The Screenwriters Lab. I got in.

No shit.

No shit.

Did you tell me you'd applied?

No, I didn't.

Congratulations.

I'm not going, Mimi said. I just decided.

Don't let me and Violet stop you.

That has nothing to do with it, Mimi said. I'm not going.

Well, Dash said. Congratulations anyway.

Dash pulled another bottle from the wine rack, this one a gift from Paula, the boss with the velvet fist. Of course the wine was vintage, French, very expensive.

Are you really going to drink *that*? Mimi heard herself saying.

We're going to drink it together. Dash held the bottle up in a scornful toast. *Viva Sundance!*

Mother love. If a gun were pointed at Violet's head and a terrible choice had to be made, who could predict how Mimi would choose? Mimi regretted not putting up a bigger fight when Violet announced she was moving in with Dash. Violet had been eleven, surly and obstinate, when she made her decision. But you don't even like your father, Mimi tried to argue.

I like him better than *you,* Violet retorted. And that was that.

And now the animal is being sent off to some crematorium upstate. And now Agnes is more than likely dead. Again Mimi flips open her cell phone—messages, one missed call, how come she didn't hear the phone ring, exciting! She punches in Carmelo's number. The opening chords of Led Zeppelin's "Black Dog" kick in. Going on for far too long, in Mimi's opinion. Then you had to wait for her brother's curt little greeting: I'm not available. Leave a message.

Mimi talks fast. Melo, listen. I've made up my mind. I'm going with you to look for Agnes, to talk to the cops, whatever we need to fucking do! And by the way? That Led Zeppelin thing is getting really *tired.*

The missed call is from a restricted number. Bobby playing one of his games, or one of the slippery hedge-fund boys, either Ivan or Matthieu. *Don't call us, we'll call you.* A rambling, awkward voice mail from Vukocevic. Hello, Mimi, it's Alex. Aleksandar Vukocevic. The stalker from the animal clinic. Please know of course that is a joke. And not a funny one, perhaps—

Mimi frowns, annoyed. She is ready to write him off, but something tells her to save the message. She will deal with it when she gets home. The text message is from Violet:

Hry! Im Strvng!

Souk

Eleanor was relieved. Ferrucci Brothers Seafood Pork & Pasta had not gone out of business. And neither had Souk, the herb-and-spice shop next door to it. The unfriendly and gargantuan Persian cat still snoozed in Souk's storefront window. As old as Eleanor in cat years. A funky PLEASE DON'T PET ME sign was taped to its wicker bed. Eleanor could see through the window that Luanne, the paranoid hippie proprietor, was gone. Replaced by a young, slender, more striking version of Luanne, sitting behind the cash register. (Spiky short hair and snazzy eyeglasses—maybe Luanne's granddaughter?) The shopgirl was engrossed in a book. She glanced up when the door opened and Eleanor walked in, then went right back to what she was reading. Attractive. Eleanor made a mental note to sneak a peek at the title of the book when it was time to pay.

And after Souk, on to Ferrucci Brothers to buy jumbo prawns (if they had any left), maybe mussels and clams. Definitely a big bottle of virgin olive oil, the best they had. She wanted to say hello to Dominic and Massimo, ask after their wives, their children and grandchildren. Eleanor had not felt this invigorated, this curious and social, in years. And the coat she was wearing—the red, opulent coat that had once belonged to Yvonne—made her feel like a fierce drag queen diva. A cliché, and brilliant.

Eleanor chose a shopping basket from the stack by the door. Souk's displays were artful, as she remembered. Lemongrass stalks sprouted from earthenware vases, red and green chili peppers filled pewter bowls. Glass jars crammed with star anise, cloves, fennel seeds, cumin, lavender, sticks of dried cinnamon. Oh, why not? Eleanor thought, wanting it all. Buy a bit of everything, replenish the bare cupboards in your kitchen, you won't regret it. Lucky old woman. She had money, more than enough. Money from the recent sale of her archives (all those photographs, handwritten letters, postcards from famous people!), money left to her by Yvonne, money from the royalty checks that still trickled in from time to time. Death was imminent; she may as well splurge.

The shopgirl put her book down. Eleanor handed her a bank card and the basket loaded with things.

In Search Of Duende. She had expected the shopgirl to be immersed in some hot new novel, but this—this was too much.

The shopgirl smiled politely at Eleanor. Debit or credit?

Debit. Are you a Lorca fan?

I'm doing my dissertation on flamenco as an act of resistance during the Spanish Civil War. Lorca's a primary source.

That's smart. Really, really smart, Eleanor said. Thinking, I am still capable of cheap flattery. And if we chat long enough, it will seem perfectly natural to invite her to my dinner party. Eleanor had always found Lorca a trifle overwrought, precious and romantic. She had argued with Mimi and Yvonne about it, but if this stalwart, snazzy young thing was another Lorca devotee . . . then what the hell.

The young woman came alive. Do you know his "Play and Theory of the Duende"?

No, Eleanor lied.

Oh, wow, you should! It's this lecture Lorca gave in Buenos Aires in

1930—no, '33!—about—and I'm sorry if I'm oversimplifying or making it sound pretentious—but it's about the struggle and state of possession that go into making great art. Duende's hard to explain. Sorta like when black singers are said to have soul. I mean, what is *soul*? Either you have duende or you don't.

Exactly, Eleanor said. Have you read Lorca in Spanish?

No. The shopgirl gave an embarrassed laugh. I can get a little earnest and reductive about this duende shit. Sorry.

Nothing to be sorry about. I'm intrigued. Eleanor was about to ask her name, but the shopgirl was suddenly all business. Paper or plastic?

Beg your pardon?

Some people prefer not to use plastic bags.

Plastic, Eleanor said.

ELEANOR DARLING! Nneka was waving to her frantically, turning heads on Bleecker Street. Benjy stood next to his beaming, insanely tall, insanely glamorous wife, looking glum. Eleanor froze. Benjy tossed his cigarette aside but made no move toward Eleanor. He still sported a beard. Mr. Marketing and Media Consultant. Mr. Branding. Constantly miserable, but clearly prosperous.

Nneka ran up to Eleanor and gave her a fierce squeeze. Eleanor reveled in the tart, woodsy scent of Nneka's perfume.

You look smashing!

No, you look smashing.

Where've you been?

Where I've always been.

Well, I've missed you!

And I've missed you.

Benjy finally sauntered over. What a sexy, gorgeous couple they made. Eleanor almost forgot that she had not been invited to their wedding.

Nneka's tone grew sharp and exasperated. Benjamin. Please? Eleanor needs help with her bags.

No, Eleanor said, stepping back. No thank you, but I don't.

Benjy's voice was cutting and cool. Is that Mum's coat?

Your friend Rajiv called me, Eleanor said, ignoring his question.

I heard.

I said yes to the reading, Eleanor said.

I heard. Benjy glanced at his watch. Nneka, the thing's at five.

Nneka ignored him. She grabbed Eleanor's hand and placed it against her belly, which was firm and flat. We're having a baby.

A *baby*? Eleanor was astonished.

I cannot wait to get FAT, Nneka said. Will you still love me, Benjamin?

More than ever, Benjy said.

If the baby's a girl, we're calling her Yvonne, Nneka said.

That's lovely, Eleanor said.

Benjy touched the small of Nneka's back. We should go.

Nneka bent to kiss Eleanor good-bye. Come visit.

Absolutely. When the baby's born.

That's such a long way away, darling. Come see us *soon*.

Eleanor turned to Benjy. You've sold your mother's place in Chinatown, haven't you? Tell me it isn't true.

Afraid it is.

But why?

Let's just say I no longer found the rodents charming, Benjy said.

Eleanor felt stunned and confused. But where do you and Nneka live? I don't even know where you *live*.

Benjy chuckled grimly. We've got a place in London. And one in Brooklyn.

Fort Greene, Nneka interjected. Come visit us in Fort Greene, Eleanor.

Absolutely, Eleanor said. When the baby's born.

She watched them walk away. A crowd started gathering on the sidewalk around her. Everyone staring at the black Hummer parked in front of the new shoe place across the street. The hulking commando type waiting beside the ostentatious vehicle glowered back at the gawking crowd. Some sort of bodyguard-chauffeur, Eleanor supposed. She was too frazzled by her encounter with Benjy and Nneka to be interested in the spectacle that was about to unfold. There was still more shopping to do at Ferrucci Brothers. *The prawns.* Should she call the whole thing off? A fucking dinner party, the Mad Hatter's dinner party, what the hell was she thinking?

There they are! Someone shoved Eleanor, hard. Someone else caught her by the arms as she was about to fall. Why, it's Lorca Girl, Eleanor remembers saying to the young woman from Souk.

To the rescue, the shopgirl said.

With Lorca Girl by her side, Eleanor felt safe and not in such a hurry to flee. A pair of wispy, golden-haired trolls in huge sunglasses emerged from the shoe place. Eleanor mistook them for children. An older woman, also in sunglasses, walked behind them, carrying their shopping bags. The driver commando held open the passenger door. The crowd—a sizable one by now—craned their necks and readied their cell phones and cameras. Their anxious, hostile energy was palpable. The older woman and the trolls scrambled into the Hummer and were driven quickly away. The crowd began to scatter.

What the hell was *that*? Eleanor asked in a weary voice.

The Olsen twins, Lorca Girl answered. Or maybe duendes. She met Eleanor's gaze. I should get back to work. You gonna be okay? Need me to put you in a taxi?

Prelude to My Life as a Horror Movie

I dreamed of running away and changing my luck for years. I was twenty-five when I finally said to myself, Now or never, Agnes. You're getting too old. I ran first to Lizard Point, then to General Johnson City, then to Manila, then Tokyo and Riyadh. I learned how to conceal my scar with thick makeup, dance naked and look indifferent. I dressed up like a French maid, sang anime karaoke, spoke Japanese and Korean. I was careless once and got pregnant. One of the girls from Orchid in Kabukichō told me where to go to get rid of it.

I met Vanessa and the doctor in Riyadh. Imagine finding a relative like Vanessa—distant, but definitely a relative—so far from home. Our resemblance to each other was uncanny, though Vanessa did not have an ugly scar on her cheek and she was curvaceous and much, much prettier than I was. Confident and outspoken, besides. Bossing her husband around with that big, naughty smile on her face. Making him laugh while he did her bidding. Making *me* laugh. I couldn't believe how my luck had changed. Vanessa and the doctor had connections at the embassy. They fixed my papers, paid for everything, and brought me back with them to the States. To take care of their plump little pair of twins and live in Dream Come True, Change My Luck, New Jersey.

Think of it as a paid vacation, Vanessa had said. But I'm getting ahead of myself.

⁂

St. Lucy's Eyes was the name of the town where I was born. Ragged, garbage-strewn mountains surrounded us, shadowy mountains where a band of rogue soldiers were said to live. You wouldn't know it except for the occasional sight of black smoke. There were fires raging and wars going on up in those mountains. People getting hacked up and dying all the time.

⁂

Sanda, my mother, stuck her hand inside herself and tried to rip me out of her womb when she was five months pregnant. She didn't get very far, sickened by the pain and the blood streaming down her legs. She called out to Albertine, who lived across the dirt road. Fortunately, Albertine was home. You could have bled to death, Albertine scolded Mother, helping her to bed. Do you want this baby or not? Sometimes I do, sometimes I don't, Mother had answered.

⁂

The humid days and nights crawled by. The weeks and months. Albertine looked in on Mother daily, to make sure that we were all right. She brought us fish and wild cabbage. Tea that tasted of red dirt. Mother refused to eat, but I was too ravenous and insistent and wouldn't let her rest until she did. We grew bigger and bigger. Night after night Mother reported for work at Infinite Technology. She was a single woman with a gigantic belly that was hard to miss, but the other workers on the assembly line couldn't be bothered. They'd seen it all before. The fatherless and unwanted children of St. Lucy's Eyes, roaming the streets in packs like wild dogs. According to Albertine, most didn't live past the age of five or six.

~

I floated in the dark, salty sea of Mother's womb, wondering when she might try to kill me again.

~

She gave birth to me at home, with only Albertine to help her. Albertine was born a man but had lived most of her life as a woman. She came from the north, high up in the mountains, where people were poorer than we were. Albertine kept her age a secret. She was small but strong, and she wore her long white hair, which smelled of coconut oil, in a thick braid down her back.

~

Drink this special soup I made, Albertine said to my mother. It will ease the pain, Sanda.

Smells like the devil's sweat. Tastes even worse.

Hold your breath and drink it down. You'll thank me later.

~

It took two days of agony before I surrendered to being born. Mother bucked and heaved and grunted, bit Albertine's hand and spoke in tongues. Water and mucus came out of her. Don't push, Albertine said. The baby's not ready. Mother crawled around the floor on all fours, howling. The

Archangel Michael swooped in through an open window and jabbed her with his fiery sword.

⁂

It was nearly midnight when Albertine finally left. Only then did Mother look at me. I lay in the crook of her arm, a lizardy girl who weighed nothing and didn't cry. Mother kept staring, as if trying to make up her mind. I puckered my lips, curled and uncurled my fists, waited for her to smother me with a pillow.

⁂

Mother gathered the strength to get out of bed, kept the lights off, and rummaged in the dark for more rags to stuff between her legs. Albertine had warned her that the bleeding could go on for days. Mother would tell me the gory details of her ordeal a few years later. I was still a child, but old enough to understand. Mother laughed softly as she talked, relishing her memories, oblivious to the horror in my eyes. *You cannot imagine, Agnes. How my self burned and throbbed, a bloody flower, an open wound.*

⁂

The night I was born, Mother scooped me off the bed, opened the front door as quietly as she could, and started walking. We stayed away from the main road and set off through a forest of charred trees to get to the river. The night swarmed with mosquitoes and bats. There was no breeze. Mother stood on the edge of the riverbank. The winding river was beautiful, polluted and deep. I made a soft, sighing sound, sensing what my mother was about to do. She started to throw me in, then hesitated. She tried to throw me in a second time. Again she lost her nerve. With a cry of rage and frustration, Mother clawed deeply at my cheek. I quivered. Let go my first pathetic sound, a whimper.

~

She turned back toward the house. I made a feeble attempt to suck at her breast. A beam of bright light, the sound of a low, familiar voice. Where have you been, Sanda? Albertine kept the flashlight aimed at us. What have you done? Why is there blood on the baby? Mother ran past Albertine into the house, bolting the door behind her. She was panting like an animal. None of your business, none of your business, none of your business.

~

The humid days and nights crawled by. The weeks and months. Mother hated me less and less. *I wanted to name you Albertine. But I was angry with her for meddling, so I named you Agnes instead. After Agnes of Rome, patron saint of young girls, rape victims, and virgin martyrs.*

~

I was a shy, brooding child who slept in the same bed as her mother. The cruel mark Mother had left on my cheek grew more pronounced as I got older. I hated and loved my face. People often remarked at how pretty I was, in spite of the scar. An accident, Mother said, to anyone who asked.

I hated and loved my mother and did everything to please her. She sent me to the only school in town, a hot, fly-infested place filled with other impoverished children who had nowhere else to go. There was one book, which we all shared. Never enough paper, or pencils to write with. An outdated map of the world was tacked on the wall. I liked staring at it while I daydreamed. Everyone daydreamed a lot, including the teachers. At the end of a long day of dreaming, we'd trudge home to our chores and secrets. I to boil rice and sweep the house and yard and do whatever else Mother expected me to do while she worked the night shift. Albertine had moved back up north. There was no one around to tell me stories. I turned on the battered transistor radio that Albertine had passed on to me before she left, hoping for a good song to come on. Something peppy, that would fill me with joy and make me dance. While I swept, I'd mouth the lyrics, pretending the voice on the radio was mine. *Let's get animal, animal . . . Let me hear your body talk, your body talk. . . .*

My father showed up at our door when I was nine years old. What do you want? Mother was scowling. He kept smiling. I stood next to my mother and stared. He was short and powerfully built, with a boxer's broken nose and thick, wavy black hair. His clothes and shoes, though dusty, didn't look cheap. He had obviously traveled a long way to see us. Mother glanced at his large, canvas shoulder bag with suspicion. You can't stay here, she said. I've brought gifts, the man said. Mother's laugh was bitter. How nice. He dabbed at the sweat on his forehead and neck with a handkerchief. Who are you? I asked him. Your father, he answered. My name is Frank. Frank, I repeated. What kind of name is that?

He stayed a week. Mother asked to be temporarily switched to a day shift so she could spend nights with him at home. I was forced to sleep outside, in a makeshift tent that Mother and Frank rigged next to the outhouse. Actually, I hardly slept. All I could think about was Frank lying in bed with my mother. Putting his thing inside her.

Every night after Mother fell asleep, Frank would sneak outside to smoke in the dark. Sometimes he would stand right by my tent. I'd hold my breath, half expecting him to bend down, look inside, and start talking to me. *Agnes, let me tell you the story of my life. Then you can tell me yours.* He never did. That Friday, while Mother was at work and I was at school, Frank left without saying good-bye.

Mother acted like she didn't care that he was gone. She went back to working the night shift at Infinite Technology. She was starting to go blind in one eye but forbade me to mention it to anyone, terrified of losing her job. The humid days and stifling nights crawled by. The weeks, the months. Frank showed up a few more times. Always without warning, always with a smile. He brought more gifts. A bottle of Johnnie Walker for Mother, a pink Hello Kitty dress and a pair of canvas Vans for me. He never stayed more than a night. During one of those visits, Frank asked for permission to take me to General Johnson, the capital city. I want Agnes to meet my sister and her family, he said. Mother was drinking whiskey and in a fighting mood. What about me? Don't you want them to meet *me*?

The day we left, I wore the Hello Kitty dress and checkered Vans. We took the bus to Lizard Point and waited for another bus that would take us to General Johnson. Frank bought me sardines, bread, banana chips, and soda from a kiosk at the bus station. Cigarettes and a pint of rum for himself. We boarded a clean, air-conditioned bus and took our seats in the back, so Frank could smoke. I wasn't used to the air-con and began to shiver. Frank made me put on his jacket. He lit a Marlboro and started bragging about Dul, his older sister, a lawyer who was married to a former lawyer turned politician named Balthazar. I wouldn't be surprised if Balthazar became our next president. That's if they don't kill him first, Frank said with a chuckle.

Why didn't you invite Mother to come with us? I asked him. Frank took his time answering the question. Your mother would feel out of place, he said. I want to get off this bus and go home, I said, starting to cry. It's too cold. Frank put his arm around me. Don't cry, Agnes. We're almost there. He poked lightly at the keloid on my cheek with his finger. How did you get that scar? An accident, I said, recoiling from his touch. Are my cousins going to make fun of me? Frank shook his head. Of course not. Do you like music, Agnes? I don't know, I said. Your cousin Carmelo is a musical prodigy. Which means he started playing the piano and reading music when he was only five years old. Imagine that. What about my cousin Mimi? Is she a prodigy? I asked. Frank shrugged. There's only room for one per family, he said. I looked out the window. Men and women on horses galloped wildly across green, watery fields of rice. It started to rain. Hey, asshole. Can't you read the signs? No smoking or drinking allowed, the driver said in a loud voice. The other passengers turned to stare at us. My father didn't budge, just took another swig of rum and kept smoking. I slid down in my seat and closed my eyes, hoping to disappear.

Dul and Balthazar's house was the biggest I'd ever seen. A palace, Frank called it. Everyone was shocked to see us, but polite. Welcome, welcome, Dul said. Frank had forgotten to tell them we were coming. There were maids in uniform and tiny dogs and birds in cages and many telephones. Two televisions and a *computer.* Teardrops of shimmering glass hung over the dining-room table, giving off heat and light. What is that? I whispered to Frank in awe. A *chandelier.* It cost almost as much as this house, Frank answered in a quiet voice. Several men—dressed alike in crisp white shirts and creased black pants—hovered on the patio. Stop staring at them, Agnes. They're your uncle's goons, Frank hissed. I couldn't help asking, Where are their guns? A little too loudly, probably. One of them overheard and gave me a sly wink. My cousins were summoned. Carmelo, the famous prodigy, was a tall, heavyset boy of fourteen. Mimi was a thin girl of nine like me. She stared at me with great curiosity. I didn't know where to look or what to do. My wrinkled Hello Kitty dress felt tacky and cheap. So this is Sanda's daughter? Dul finally said. She was a slender woman, with kind eyes and the same thick, black, wavy hair as my father's. Balthazar wore eyeglasses and seemed a serious and preoccupied man, not too pleased by having unexpected guests. I don't think he liked my father very much, though he shook his hand. Well, Frank. You're lucky we were home, Balthazar said.

~

It felt wrong to call them "Uncle Balthazar" and "Aunt Dul." The same way it felt wrong to call Frank "Papa." I couldn't do it.

~

Dul had the maid order KFC for dinner. Buckets and buckets of it, with rice and mashed potatoes and gravy on the side. Coca-Cola with ice. Beer and wine. Then we had three kinds of ice cream. Rocky Road, Purple Yam, Mango Delite. I ate and ate until there was nothing left. Is this your first KFC? Your first ice cream? Mimi asked me in English. She had a smirk on her face. Don't be rude, Dul admonished her sharply. Then she added: Especially to your cousin. There were no more buses running until the next afternoon. Of course you should spend the night, Dul said. Of course, said Balthazar. My father got the guest room, while I was to sleep on one of the twin beds in Mimi's room. Loan Agnes something to sleep in, Dul said to Mimi. Mimi frowned but didn't say anything. Dul bent down so we could each give her a kiss. *Good night, girls. Don't forget to say your prayers.* I was terrified of being left alone with my bossy, insolent cousin. She disappeared into her bathroom (she had her own bathroom! a toilet that flushed!) and came out wearing a giant Michael Jackson T-shirt that came down past her knees. Why don't you just sleep in your dress? It looks really comfortable, Mimi said. If you want me to, I said meekly, which made her laugh. I was just testing you, stupid. She pulled open one of the drawers in her bureau, dug out a frilly nightgown that had seen better days, and handed it to me with a smile. If you tell me how you got that scar on your cheek, I'll let you watch *Sailor Moon* on my VCR.

~

My father took me to see my cousins two more times before dropping out of our lives once and for all. I don't know why I agreed to go. Mimi hated having to spend time with me. You're so weird, Agnes. You just sit there, with nothing to say. Carmelo was kinder. He once caught me spying on him while he played the piano. I can teach you about music, he said.

Mother and I heard about the bomb that exploded in the city of General Johnson from a man on the radio. A rally in the market plaza had been organized by the PPPR—People's Party for Progress and Reform. The bomb was planted in one of the stalls close to the stage. Balthazar was in the middle of a speech when it went off. A stirring speech, said the man on the radio. Dul had been sitting behind him, with the other candidates and their wives. The bomb was huge and powerful, full of nails. Everyone was killed, and the market was in flames. I wonder if your father was there, was all Mother managed to say.

I dropped out of school when I was fifteen. Mother got me hired at Infinite Technology assembling microchips. We needed the extra money so Mother could travel to General Johnson and see a specialist about her eye. The humid days and stifling nights crawled by. The weeks, the months. One afternoon I came home from work and found a letter from my father lying on our doorstep. Frank wrote that he was now married to an American woman. They lived in Colma, California, and he had no plans of coming back. *I love you, dear Agnes. You are my blood, and I miss you very much.* What was the American woman's name? Where was Colma, California? His Stateside phone number was written next to his signature. *Just in case you need me.* I had to laugh. Frank must have lost his mind, since he knew that Mother and I didn't own a phone. I started to tear up the letter, but something told me to keep it. I hid it in the bottom of my shoulder bag, which I took with me wherever I went. I never told my mother. For all she knew, Frank was dead.

Everyone said he was no good, but I fell in love with Shakespeare anyway. What did I care that he was much too old for me, that he lived with a sour-faced woman he called his wife, that he was known to beat her when he was drunk, that they had many children and he beat them, too?

Sometimes I dreamed of running away with him, sometimes I dreamed of running away by myself.

~

I finally found the courage when I turned twenty-five. Now or never, Agnes. You're getting too old. Stealing from Mother was so easy it almost broke my heart. She made no secret of hiding what little money she had in a biscuit tin under our bed. *When I die, this money will be yours. . . .* But of course Mother didn't die.

~

It had been raining for a week. Winds gusting at a hundred miles an hour. The floor of our little house buckled, and the tin roof caved in. Everything stank of mildew and rot. By the second week, there were power outages, incidents of looting around town, outbreaks of dysentery and cholera. Yet Infinite Technology—a concrete fortress built on high ground to withstand nature's catastrophes—remained in full operation, its generators humming merrily away. Mother and I, along with all the other downtrodden IT employees, were expected to show up and work our usual shifts. When the river flooded, IT dispatched an emergency fleet of inflatable boats to ferry workers to and from the plant.

~

The rain slackened a bit on the day of my escape. I refused to get out of bed and pretended to have the flu. Everything hurts, I groaned. Mother laid a hand on my forehead. At least you don't have a fever. Hurry and get dressed. The boat will be here soon. We don't want to be late. I'm too sick to go to work, I said. They'll dock your pay, Mother said. Or replace you. And me. We're lucky to have jobs, Agnes.

~

My tears looked real. What could Mother do but get on that boat and go to work by herself? *Now or never, Agnes.* I put on my clothes, made the sign of the cross, and got on my knees, begging God to forgive me as I reached under the bed for the tin box. I stuffed the money next to my father's letter at the bottom of my shoulder bag, which looked like leather but was really plastic and—I prayed—waterproof.

~

The Road of Massacred Innocents was the town's only connection to the highway and General Johnson beyond. I knew that the road was gone, replaced by a muddy sea of floating trees and dead things. But I went there anyway and stood on a soggy embankment, waiting. If I were patient and prayed, something good would happen. In a soft voice, I sang to myself:

Milkfish / peanut / coconut /
Agnes's little bushel /
Agnes's little hut /
eggplant / okra / purple yam /
the rooster's crowing /
he's too impatient /
the goat's by the river /
wondering where I am

The sound of a sputtering motor silenced me. I crouched in the tall, prickly grass jutting out from the embankment. A long wooden boat painted many colors came slowly around the bend. I sighed with relief. Shakespeare sat at the forward end. An old man, tattooed from head to toe, squatted by the motor on the back end. The most voluptuous and popular whore at Comfort Spa sat between them. Her name was Tiny. Tiny's son, Darling, a boy of two, sat on her lap. Have you lost your mind, Agnes? Shakespeare stared at me, amazed. I held the bag high and waded out to the boat. The water was deeper than I thought it would be, swampy and full of twigs, rocks, and shards of glass that got in the way. If I had to swim, I would.

Crazy woman. The devilish grin on Shakespeare's face made me blush. He had gotten me alone and drunk on his boat more than once. Shakespeare would paw at me, going on about how pretty I was. Prettier than his wife, prettier than Tiny, prettier than all the pretty whores at Comfort Spa. He'd trace the scar on my cheek with the tip of his finger. It makes you more beautiful, he'd say. Then we'd kiss. Sometimes he reeked of fish. Sometimes of cigarettes and other women.

I hoisted myself onto the boat, almost tipping it over. There are too many of us, and we're all going to drown in this water! Filthy, filthy water! Tiny shrieked. Shut up, or I'll throw you and that fucking kid off this boat! Shakespeare yelled. Darling burst out crying and hid his face in his mother's ample bosom. Tiny attempted to comfort the child and patted him on the back, glancing nervously at Shakespeare. The boy would not stop crying. May I hold him? I asked her. The boy stiffened and kept wailing but then slowly relaxed in my arms. He finally quieted down. What a sweet, pretty boy you are, I cooed. You're good with children, Tiny said with a forlorn smile.

The boat moved through the main part of town, past what used to be the mayor's fancy house (a dog barked at us from the mayor's roof), past what used to be the Temple of St. Lucy's Eyes, past Comfort Spa & Massage, Rudy's Unisex Hair, past the old schoolhouse and all that remained of the Tasty Yummy Bakery. Tiny suddenly came alive. That's my mother's place. Stop so I can get off! Your mother's been evacuated,

Shakespeare said. I've told you that a thousand times. Can't you see? Nothing's left. I want to see for myself, Tiny said.

Shakespeare signaled the old man to kill the motor. Keep your shoes on before getting in the water, I warned her. Tiny lifted her ruffled skirt of glittering mirrors and carefully lowered herself into the murky water, which came up to her neck. I handed Tiny her child. Holding the boy high above her head, Tiny waded toward the partially submerged bakery. Crazy woman. Shakespeare shook his head in disgust. The old man spit in the water and started the motor.

I was sorry to see her go. What's going to happen to them? I asked. Shakespeare gave an impatient shrug. We retreated into a world of silence, except for the sputtering motor and the screeching of a solitary hawk circling the skies. The huge, stinking corpse of—I thought it was a man—bobbed in the water, so bloated it was about to burst. No one said anything. Then came a wounded horse trapped in a tangle of fallen trees, eyes bulging in panic. Screaming as only a horse could. Do something! I grabbed Shakespeare by the arm. Stop looking at it, Shakespeare said, pulling a .45 from underneath his shirt. He shot the thrashing horse between the eyes. The sound was deafening.

The boat moved past the massive iron gates of Infinite Technology. I gave a somber little wave to my mother inside. I felt a twinge of shame and remorse, knowing that she was hard at work, that she was going blind, that I might never see her again.

Can you take me to Lizard Point? I asked Shakespeare. Too far, Agnes. Not enough fuel. I have to catch a bus, I said. Shakespeare's tone was scornful. And where do you think you're going in a *bus*? To General Johnson, I answered. I'll look for a job. Get my own place. Then maybe I'll go somewhere else, get a better job and a bigger place. Then maybe, who knows? Shakespeare laughed. Stop dreaming, Agnes. I have money, I said quietly. I can pay for the extra fuel.

Beast in the Mirror

Violet puffed away on her last rolled Drum as she studied her reflection in the faux-antique mirror. Which her parents—when they were still together—had found dumped on a sidewalk in Chinatown. The full-length mirror—with its cheap wooden frame painted a tarnished gold—was one of a handful of things Mimi didn't get rid of after the breakup. Weird, Violet thought. *Très, très* weird. She lifted her arm and struck an angular pose, her facial expression sultry and remote. Like Karmen Pedaru in that hot Rodarte dress in the last issue of *W.* Violet could see herself in it—a dress that didn't look finished, that was tattered and full of holes and cost something in the vicinity of *eight thousand dollars.* Violet puckered her lips and blew circles of smoke at the mirror. She was trying not to think about her current sucky situation. Ten pounds overweight, failing nearly everything at school, always broke. She hated being so utterly dependent on the largesse of dear ol' Mom and Dad, so at their mercy, so fucking *enslaved.* And why were the last ten pounds always the hardest to lose? When she turned eighteen . . .

She saw herself on the beach in Santa Monica, accepting the Independent Spirit Award for Best Director in the Rodarte dress and her cowboy boots. Or maybe Sundance. Where she would be the youngest and only director to ever win all the prizes at once—the Grand Jury Prize, the U.S. Directing Award, and the Audience Award. Except at Sundance she'd definitely have to wear her North Face over the fragile little dress. Violet might even bring her mother as her date, maybe acknowledge Mimi from the podium as she smiled and gave her witty speech. The audience would cheer and applaud, suddenly realizing who Mimi was. *Stand up, Mom!*

Her father had offered to pay for a haircut but was always short of cash. Probably blew it all on that little shipment from Mexico. Violet knew that once she moved back in with her mother, Dash was going to stop being so generous. She sighed. How she longed to have money of her own. Maybe she should go into partnership with Charlie and deal acid or coke or E at school. Except Charlie was a reluctant dealer, jumpy and paranoid about getting caught. She did not like the idea of getting busted and thrown in some juvenile-detention facility upstate, getting gang-raped with a broomstick by a bunch of sadistic prison guards with nothing better to do. So maybe a regular baby-sitting job made more sense, like Kenya had. Except babies were a drag. So maybe Starbucks. Patrice, Kenya's older sister, worked the one by Lincoln Center and made okay tips. And the one thing Violet knew was how to make an excellent cup of espresso. She could see herself as a barista, but did Starbucks hire fourteen-year-olds?

New zit on her chin. Inflamed, gross. Maybe a fucking boil or something. This always happened right before her period. *Period.* What a dumb word for blood gushing out of your vagina every month. Her mother was right. Sometimes English just didn't cut it.

First things first. The funky vintage look had to go, the cowboy boots and frumpy thrift-store dresses that stank of mothballs even if you washed them a hundred times. She needed a serious makeover, needed to change her life, maybe kill herself, maybe hook up, enough already with this virgin shit, she should hook up with Omar or Charlie. Charlie was one of her two best friends (Kenya being the other), truly sweet and truly sexy. And gay. Or so he said. Always striving to be outrageous and *different*. Violet didn't care. She was smitten the moment she first laid eyes on him. Mr. Pavino's class. Global History. Part One: The Egyptians.

Beast in the mirror. On its back, claws in the air. Smoke.

Violet was a baby then, but she remembers the day Dash and Mimi found the mirror on Doyers Street. Remembers the day vividly, as if. How bright and brisk and clear, perfect for a stroll. I remember the weirdest shit. Like being *born,* she once confessed to Kenya and Omar and Charlie when they were high. Bethanne may have been there, too. They were in Charlie's room, lying next to one another on Charlie's king-size bed, listening to Manu Chao, to Violet describe her dreams and brag about her special powers, laughing hysterically at nothing. At one point Charlie got up and began to dance in exquisite slow motion. Omar grabbed Charlie, and they kissed. Violet remembers that all the girls were giggling, finding it all strangely beautiful and . . . well, *hot.*

Her parents were young. Dashiell tall and aloof, Mimi still flabby from having been pregnant. Violet remembers her mother not being her usual grumpy, preoccupied self that day. Remembers how carefully her father navigated the secondhand baby carriage through the narrow, teeming streets crammed with jabbering women doing their Sunday shopping. Remembers being four months old, awake and alert in her carriage. It was her mother who spotted the mirror. Violet remembers the fishy stench from the bagged-up trash piled near the curb. Remembers her mother calling out to her father. *Dashiell . . .*

Her father slipped the heavy mirror on top of her folded-up carriage in the trunk of a cab. Violet remembers how her mother held her close on the bumpy ride home, remembers being jostled as her mother suddenly leaned over to plant an unexpected kiss on her father's mouth. *As if.* In love, if love, were they ever?

Violet remembers being five years old and waking up to the beast howling in the alley outside her bedroom window. It was raining hard, and she didn't want to go to school. She hated school, hated being around rude, giant, stinky kids who loomed over her and made ugly faces. She remembers refusing to get dressed. Standing in the middle of her room in her frilly panties, sobbing. Her sobs almost as loud as the beast's mournful howling. Her parents argued in the kitchen about Violet's behavior, about money. Then her father left, slamming the door behind him. The beast was suddenly silent, and Violet grew silent. She peered out the window, saw nothing but sheets of rain. Her mother stood in the doorway of her bedroom and began pleading with her. Mama has to go see someone important, Violet.

Is it the doctor?

No. It's about work.

Movie work, Violet remembers herself saying.

Yes, her mother said, smiling. Movie work. But if you don't get dressed and cooperate—

There's a monster in the alley, Violet said.

Violet and her mother were waiting to cross the street when the animal started howling again. Violet let go of her mother's hand and ran out from beneath the umbrella. Her mother chased after her, shouting, *Be careful!* Violet approached the drenched and cowering animal. Its right ear was torn off and bleeding. The animal growled and hissed but didn't flee. We've got to save it, Violet said.

She was picking at the red, angry-looking zit when her mother walked in with a bag from Whole Foods. *Whole Foods?* Violet tried not to sound too disappointed.

Eggplant and goat cheese, Mimi said. On ciabatta.

But I wanted bacon, Violet said.

I thought you didn't eat meat.

I love the way you make bacon, Violet said.

If you don't want the fucking sandwich— Mimi's arm was throbbing.

She slipped off her jacket and let it fall to the floor. What she needed was a goddamn nap.

I WANT IT. Violet grabbed the bag and sat down at the dining table. She tore open the sandwich wrapping and began to eat. Mimi sat across from her and watched.

Wow, Mimi said.

Wow what? Violet defensive, chewing away.

Would you like a plate?

Violet grunted and shook her head. The sandwich gone in a flash. Violet burped. Eleanor came by, she said. All dressed up. We're invited over later for dinner. I don't want to go.

Eleanor's a good cook.

I don't care, Violet said. She stared at her mother's arm. 'Sup with those bandages?

It's nothing, Mimi said. The vet insisted on fixing it. After a pause, she said, He asked me out.

Ewww. Violet was not in the mood to hear about her mother's sex life or some creepy potential suitor. I wanna be a vet. Don't you think I'd be good at it?

Yes, Mimi said. I actually do.

I called Dashiell. Told him I was staying with you.

Mimi waited. Dash was a volatile subject between them. She knew she had to be careful.

He was pissed, Violet continued. Tried not to show it. Acting all cool and stuff.

Mimi made an effort to sound gentle. You sure about coming to live with me?

You're my mother, Violet said.

She was not finished, following Mimi into the bedroom, sitting on the edge of Mimi's bed as Mimi kicked off her shoes and lay down to rest. And by the way? Uncle Carmelo called my cell. Said he's been trying to reach you. Said why bother having a cell if you never have it on? Started shouting all this stuff, like it was my fault, really fucking psycho. I wish—I really wish you'd stop giving out my number!

I'm sorry he upset you.

I didn't understand what he was shouting. It wasn't even *English*!

Your uncle gets very emotional, Mimi murmured, closing her eyes. I'm sure he didn't mean to—

HE DID. Violet waited for a response that never came. Her mother had finally succumbed to her exhaustion. Violet sat on the edge of the bed and watched her mother sleep. Mimi lay on her back, hands clasped and resting on her stomach, mouth slightly open. Her dark, unruly hair fanned out on the pillow. She looked dead.

Jaguar

Ixtlala was where I met and fell in love with Yvonne. I was old when I first laid eyes on her. Not old old like I am now, but old enough to worry about making a fool of myself. Yvonne was twenty years younger, a restless beauty with terrifying eyes, a strong face and body, full of life. Thirty-five to my fifty-five, if you must know. I always thought she would outlive me. I always thought a lot of people I cherished would outlive me, as a matter of fact.

~

IXT-LA-LA.

What exactly does it mean? I asked Felix Montoya.

At one point in my life, I had spent a lot of time in Mexico, but the town of Ixtlala was new to me. A tourist destination high up in the mountains, approximately 23,175 inhabitants, one of its most prominent being *moi,* Felix said. He was toying with me, having a high old time.

Felix, please.

Ixtlala is impossible to translate into English.

Try, I said.

Serpent of the Starry Sky. Land of Mirrors. River of Tears and Eternal Remorse. Take your pick, Eleanor.

Poetic.

It's the Aztec in me, darling.

It was my first day there, and the altitude was giving me a headache. Felix wanted to show off by taking me to La Fonda, a former colonial hacienda that had been converted into a restaurant. It was his favorite place, he said. The service was impeccable. The food was to die for. I remember we had to dress up. We sat in the courtyard, knocking back shot after shot of pricey tequila reposado and sangritas. We were supposed to be having lunch. Solemn waiters hovered close by, anticipating our every need. Birds trilled in the lush, vibrant foliage. The sun was shining, the baroque fountain in the center of the courtyard gurgling merrily away.

I feel like I'm in a movie, I said, trying to ignore the dull, persistent pain in my temples.

You're not, Felix said, giving me one of those cryptic smiles. The walls are splattered with blood and too much history. But the waiters are sexy and cute, no? The young ones anyway. He scanned the glossy, oversize menu. You must be starved. We should order some chilled pomegranate soup to start. Specialty of the house.

Felix gestured for a waiter. Rattled off a list of delicacies: Chilled pomegranate soup, followed by grilled shrimp and squash blossoms. The inevitable guacamole, freshly made before us on a heavy *molcajete* made of black stone. A basket of steaming, tiny tortillas. *How's the new book coming along?*

That's a deadly question for a writer, answered Felix, downing the last of his tequila. Let's talk about your love life instead.

~

Unrequited: Vicky Gantner (elementary school), Nan (I forget her last name, but I can still see her face), Moss Blake (Yes, Moss Blake. I'll admit I found him attractive. Didn't you?).

Loves: Jocanda, Cleo, Annie, Dominique.

~

That's all? You've been very selective, Felix said. And now?

I'm on the prowl. *Did you invite Jocanda to my reading?*

Of course. But Mexico City's a long way away.

She won't come.

She is old and she is frail, Felix said. Not the Jocanda you used to know. Is fine, Eleanor. You are, as you say, on the prowl.

The town of Ixtlala was famous for its shamans and dream weavers and gringo expats and scorpions and packs of stray dogs and a spooky little pyramid tucked away in a nearby forest. Felix used to say that the forest was also home to an enigmatic, solitary jaguar. If you stay up late, Eleanor, you might get lucky and hear the jaguar's howl. A howl like no other, he said. Felix was a firm believer in the spirit world. It was one of the beliefs we shared, though I didn't bitch and moan and brag about it like he did. Felix claimed that he'd not only heard the jaguar, he'd *seen* it. Of course, he was on a three-day peyote bender at the time. The old shaman Don Rufo had been with him, acting as his spiritual guide. So had Don Rufo's wife, Susanna, a renowned weaver who went by the title Mother of All Dreams. They, too, saw the jaguar.

Mexico was my first real lover. And as with all lovers, my relationship to it is complicated. I wasn't sure I wanted to return to Mexico, but at the same time I couldn't wait to be there again. Felix had planned it so that I would arrive right before the Day of the Dead. He understood it was my kind of party. Skeletons of wood and papier-mâché, stacks of glittering sugar skulls everywhere you looked. The air perfumed with the pungent smell of marigolds, chocolate, copal incense, bloody meat.

Of course I stayed with Felix. His house was painted a vivid pink, crammed with books and paintings, pre-Columbian artifacts and back issues of *Blueboy* and the *New Yorker.* It was lovely but a little too private, located at the far end of town on a steep, winding road that ran all the way down to the market. Felix had assembled his own Day of the Dead altar in the living room. Seashells, candles, a toy airplane, a bowl of fruit, a bottle of tequila reposado, and a vase filled with orange marigolds were set before framed sepia photographs of his deceased grandparents and parents and a framed snapshot of his younger sister, Alma, who had drowned while swimming in the ocean at the age of fourteen. In the center was a black-and-white portrait of Felix's great love, the Argentine poet Guillermo Ford. Ford had lived with Felix from the age of twenty until his death in a fiery plane crash over the Andes at forty-five. Felix flew to Buenos Aires to identify and claim Guillermo's body, since Guillermo's fascist family wanted nothing more to do with their faggot poet of a son. Felix described what was left of Guillermo as "a slab of black coal."

But don't get me wrong. Ixtlala's macabre atmosphere suited me fine. I've been thinking about death all my life; I've never been afraid of it. Dry your tears, dispense with the grief, and throw a party. Bring on the mariachis, the boleros, and tequila. Get ready for the cleaning of graves, the singing, the sweets. Let us all die Mexican.

What the hell. I was so happy hanging out with Felix in Ixtlala, I went a little crazy and drank and ate too much while I was there. Ran into my fair share of shamans and stray dogs but never made it to the spooky pyramid. The only scorpion I came across was a goofy totem made of beaten copper, installed to look like it was crawling up the side of someone's house. Every time I walked down to the plaza, I'd pause to look at it.

So who lives in that house? I finally asked Felix.

A pair of unhappy artists.

And?

And nothing.

We were drinking mezcal and snorting some really fine cocaine that Ángel had scored at my behest. Actually, Felix stuck to mezcal and abstained from the powder. He hated coke. He considered it a nasty, insidious drug and—having given up on me long ago—kept lecturing Ángel about its evils. Ángel Miranda was Felix's new find—a gorgeous, moody nineteen-year-old college dropout and former waiter at La Fonda—with bright, hungry eyes and a stocky, muscular swimmer's body. Fat, balding Felix was obsessed. So much so that he'd gone on a crash diet and was seriously considering hair transplants and a face-lift. Felix certainly had the money to spend on surgical improvements. He joked with me once about wanting to adopt Ángel. *I want to take care of him, even after I'm gone.* It was no fun watching a brilliant, tough-minded writer swoon over a little hustler. No fun at all. But I was the perfect houseguest and kept my mouth shut. Besides, Ángel Miranda had proved that he could be useful to me.

The boy snatched the rolled-up bill from my hand with the most charming of smiles and helped himself to a couple of lines. Don't overdo it, *amor.* Remember the last time? Felix chided him.

Ángel did another.

Felix rolled his eyes at me. Would you believe what I have to put up with? The boy never listens.

Ángel wiped his nose with his wrist and gazed at Felix with contempt. And you, old man. You never shut up, he said.

On my last day there, I wandered through the market in a melancholy daze. Purchased a little female skeleton for myself, which I still have. I call her Eleanor. She sits at a typewriter with a forlorn expression, badly in need of a bump or a drink. I bought a splendid bottle of tequila as a gift for Felix. A token, since Felix already had many splendid bottles of tequila in his possession. I was taking him to La Fonda later that evening. A good-bye and thank-you dinner. There was a lot to be thankful for. Felix—because of his literary stature—had secured quite a bit of government funding for my reading. I was flown in, fussed over, and paid much too much.

My reading took place in the grand and gloomy Ixtlala Cultural Museum, a former sixteenth-century convent for Carmelite nuns. When Felix and I arrived, every seat was already taken. All the expats in town had decided to show up, along with the local artists and curious museum regulars. I started to panic. I can't believe it, I said to Felix. There's an audience. Felix rolled his eyes. I read the opening chapter of *Little Deaths* and excerpts from *Eyes of a Jaguar,* my voice quavering. I could feel everyone in the room looking at me and listening, listening hard. The applause after I read seemed sincere and went on for a long time.

A group of sultry young vixens approached me afterward. They had taken the bus all the way from Mexico City. We are former students of Jocanda Fox, the most butch-looking one said to me in English. We have studied your work. *How I wish Jocanda were here. How I wish you could have dragged her along.* The butch girl smiled. She had a round, adorable face and dark, slanted eyes. I asked her name. Chiqui Rosa, she said. I apologized for not speaking better Spanish and flirted—shamelessly—with Chiqui Rosa and her pals. The girls were courteous and attentive, but I think they found me rather crass. Felix brought me a drink and a little dish of God-knows-what. Miniature flautas. Mango chunks on toothpicks.

There's someone in this room, I said. I feel the heat. Her energy.

Of course you do, Felix said. You're on the prowl.

Everyone brought copies of my books for me to sign. I was too busy to notice Ángel saunter in. You're late, Felix said. Is there any food left? Ángel asked with one of those endearing smiles. Clearly he was only interested in the lavish reception. He munched on canapés and helped himself to the fruit punch spiked with tequila and ignored us both. Felix had not eaten a thing and was quite drunk and furious by the time we left. We headed home in his old Mercedes. Ángel took the wheel. Well, I said, to no one in particular. I guess my reading was a big success. Felix let me have it. Why shouldn't it be? You're my *guest.* Did you expect me to fuck things up? You've got it all wrong when it comes to my country, Eleanor. Fiestas! Sugar skulls! Frida Kahlo! You think that's all there is? That we're a bunch of happy *children*? That we don't *read*?

Your country? Why not *our* country? I said.

Chinga a tu madre, Felix muttered before passing out.

Same to you, and shame on you, Felix Montoya, I said.

Ángel snickered and kept driving.

My last day in Ixtlala, I left the market and walked slowly up the hill toward Felix's house. Savoring every step on that hot, dusty road, in no rush at all. I paused before the high adobe wall. The copper scorpion glistened in the late-afternoon sun. Next to the wooden gate was a little buzzer. I pressed the buzzer and waited. A dog began barking. The barking grew frenzied as the animal ran up to the gate. Then came the sharp voice of a woman, shouting in English. Tin-Tan! Benjamin! For godsake!

I could hear the dog panting on the other side of the gate. So close. Sorry to disturb you, I said. But it's about the scorpion.

What about it? The gate flew open. A woman glared at me with gray-green eyes. Then she smiled. One of those arrogant, knowing smiles, instantly captivating. Well, well. This is an honor.

I'm Eleanor.

Delacroix, I know. I was at your reading.

I've passed that scorpion every day, wondering who made it.

I did.

You must get a lot of unwanted visitors.

Well, you're not one of them. The woman extended a muddy hand. I'm Yvonne. Yvonne Wilder. Sorry, but I've been gardening. Please. Won't you come in?

She closed the gate behind me. A delicate, pretty child with long, curly hair—Benjamin, I assumed—held on to the collar of a burly mastiff.

Take Tin-Tan inside, Benjamin. Now.

Who's that?

Her name's Eleanor, and it's *she,* not *that.* Benjy, please. The dog. We don't want him biting our guest.

Benjamin scowled. He won't.

Benjamin. Yvonne crossed her tanned arms.

With great reluctance the child led Tin-Tan away.

Yours? I nodded toward the black basalt fountain in the garden. Water spouted from the open mouth of a lizard.

Sebastian's. My—then she corrected herself. Benjamin's father.

A pair of unhappy artists. Everything fell into place.

Anyway. Painting's more my thing, Yvonne said.

May I see them? Your paintings, I mean.

There's nothing to see. They're in storage.

I followed Yvonne into the large, airy house, which was hidden behind a cluster of flowering trees. I saw you the other night, I said to her.

You *saw* me?

Actually, I felt you in the room. You came late, sat in the back.

Wish I'd known, she said. I loved your reading.

Really?

It was your voice. Hearing the uncertainty in it and then . . . It was interesting how it suddenly changed and became so strong. I was going to stay for the reception, but . . .

Yvonne shrugged. It was a long, loaded moment of staring.

I should go, I said. I need to pack.

Leaving us so soon?

Yup.

Have a drink first, Yvonne said. I've got some fabulous mezcal. Felix says you can outdrink anybody. Outdrink him.

What a gossip, I remember saying with a laugh.

I followed Yvonne into the kitchen and watched her rinse the dirt off her hands. The cook—a plump young coquette whose name escapes me now—turned away from the stove and gave me a shy smile. Let's go upstairs, Yvonne said. Upstairs meant her bedroom and terrace, which overlooked the valley of Ixtlala. Nice view, I said. The temperature had dropped considerably. Yvonne rummaged through the drawers of a big, heavy armoire for one of her shawls. *Here, put this around you.* We sat outside and watched the sun disappear behind the mountains. It grew dark very fast. Yvonne lit citronella candles to ward off mosquitoes. The cook brought up a tray with a bottle of mezcal, a dish of cut-up limes and salt, and two shot glasses. After she left, Yvonne poured us a round.

You working on a new book? she asked, making me wince.

I have to say, I really hate that question.

So do I. But I couldn't help asking.

Why?

I'm a fan.

You're not the fan type, I said. We drank and smoked cigarettes, pretending to be enthralled by the spectacular view.

Where's your husband?

Living across town with his girlfriend.

Fuck. I'm sorry.

Nothing to be sorry about, she said.

After a pause I said, You seem pretty calm about it.

She gave another one of those dismissive shrugs. It would be hypocritical of me to flip out. I mean, I'm no saint. Sebastian and I—we decided it was better if he left. For Benjy's sake. Just a sec— She disappeared into the bedroom and came back waving a big, fat joint. Care to join me?

Nope.

Yvonne sat down and fired up. Not your drug of choice?

Nope.

The marijuana smelled powerful. I watched her body relax in the chair. She took two more tokes, then put the joint out. This stuff is dangerous, she said with a crooked smile. So whaddaya think, Eleanor?

New York? Chicago? Or maybe I should stay in Mexico. Get my own place. Build a sweat lodge. Fan myself with branches of sage.

I don't follow.

We're selling this lovely abode. *Vaya con Dios.* See ya later, alligator. Time for me to split.

And Benjamin?

My son goes where I go.

Sorry. I didn't mean—

Stop with that "sorry" shit! Yvonne was in a fury. Agitated. Beautiful.

I got up from my seat. Listen. I should go. Felix is waiting.

She grabbed my hand. Stay. Have dinner with us. I'll invite Felix. Why not? He's an old pal.

Not a good idea.

But the fun's just begun. Her face was raw and full of pain.

You're high, kiddo.

So?

Well, at the risk of pissing you off, I'll admit that I'd like nothing better than to fuck you all night until you scream. In fact, this might be love at first sight. But I've got a date with Felix and—

She burst out laughing. I expected you to be more poetic.

Ever been with a woman?

Her eyes narrowed. Does it matter?

Depends. What do you want?

That's an interesting question, Yvonne said.

I held her face with both my hands. Looked deep into her glorious, stoned eyes and kissed her. Let me call Felix and explain, she murmured. I had my hand inside her shirt. Never mind Felix, I said. She was not wearing a bra, and we were being very indiscreet. At any moment the child could walk in. She pushed me away and went back into the bedroom, closing the door behind her. I helped myself to another shot. A few minutes later, Yvonne reappeared, triumphant.

Felix declined my invitation.

Really?

He wants to hang out with that new boyfriend of his. Can't say I blame him. I promised to drive you home.

Ángel's bad news.

So what? He's young and hot. Felix deserves a little joy and pleasure, don't you think?

What about you?

About as fucked up as you are, lady.

We heard the boy come up the stairs. *Time to eat, Mum.* In the dining room, a massive red table of carved madera de narra—another one of her husband's pieces—was set for three people. We sat down. The meal was simple and sexy and elegant. Corn soup. A roast chicken. Avocados and lime. Everything tasted incredible. Tasted sexy. I couldn't stop thinking of sex. Tin-Tan curled up under the table, by Benjamin's feet, and let out a weary groan.

Does your dog really bite? I asked.

He's vicious and brave and loves me and me only, Benjamin boasted. He turned to Yvonne. Isn't that so, Mum? Tell her it's *true.*

True, Yvonne said.

That's pretty cool, I said. I'd want a dog like Tin-Tan if I were a kid.

Well you're not, the boy said.

I wanted Benjamin to like me, and not just because he was her son. There was a sweetness and a melancholy about him. I don't presume that children are naturally sweet and kind, but Benjamin was. Sweet and kind to his mother, to Tin-Tan, to the flirty cook whose name was Yoly or Yerma or something like that—it's goddamn frustrating, it's goddamn pissing me off how vividly I can recall details of that young cook's face (which was heart-shaped, with a sexy little mole on the left side, right above her lip) but not her name.

Well, anyway. *Benjamin.*

He finished eating and turned once again to his mother. Is Eleanor spending the night?

Why don't you ask her? Yvonne said.

'Cause I don't want to.

I forced myself to smile. Benjamin—you know your mother's friend, Felix Montoya?

Benjamin gave a solemn nod.

Well, he's my friend, too. And I'm spending the night at *his* house.

Benjamin looked as if he didn't believe me.

He did not want to go to bed. He thought of every excuse—including going down to the market to buy more candy to hand out to the children of Ixtlala who would be coming around with their plastic skull baskets. When Yvonne gently reminded him that there was already plenty of candy in the house, and furthermore the market wasn't open at night, Benjamin burst into tears. The cook rushed out of the kitchen. *Qué pobrecito,* she kept murmuring as she stood by helplessly. Yvonne scooped Benjamin up and carried him to bed. I'll read you a story, Benjy. I don't want a story! Benjamin wailed, kicking and thrashing in her arms. I hate you. I want Papa!

Papa's not here. So you're just gonna have to deal with me, buddy. Yvonne shut the door to his bedroom.

I brought my coffee upstairs and waited for her on the terrace. The muffled sounds of the child crying and Yvonne attempting to comfort him drifted up from below. I could not make out what Yvonne was saying. I looked around for the half-smoked joint. I wanted to get stoned, to stop worrying about what I was doing in this stranger's house. A van was coming at the crack of dawn to take me to the airport in Mexico City. But who really cared if I missed my plane? There was no one waiting in New York. Time before time. Yvonne so close, so long ago. The crying in the house finally subsided. I wrapped the shawl tighter around me and looked down into the garden. Black. Everything was black, even the trees. I felt the heat of a jaguar's curious, indifferent gaze. The black, balmy silence of night. *Eleanor?* I heard my name and didn't move, waiting for the creature to howl.

The Duende Speaks

Ladies and gentlemen, the Widow Eleanor will never cook again. Not a complicated, pretentious meal like the widow's attempting to cook tonight anyway. And for what? Watch the widow grimace while she shakes out her stiff, aching fingers. Watch how humiliating it is, this business of being old and alone. Not being able to operate a fucking can opener or uncork a wine bottle without weeping in angry frustration. Angry all the time! Where was the music and what the hell was E thinking, organizing another last-minute dinner party? She should've hired that humorless, stout little Serb—what was her name? *Mattia*—to help out for the evening. Stocky, impenetrable Mattia, who helped her wipe Yvonne's ass, change Yvonne's diapers, and give Yvonne morphine and Dilaudid, or whatever other sweet, soothing poisons the doctors might have prescribed. But with Y out of the way, E's back to her old habits. E the widow, always showing off, flirting with bookish shopgirls and killing herself over some dumb dinner party that means nothing at all. And for what? Anyway, even if Eleanor had tried, she wouldn't have found Mattia. The Slavic witch had never been one of those grateful "I like to be in America"–type immigrants. She pined for her beloved fucking Belgrade and never bothered to unpack her battered suitcases the entire time she was here. It's only been, what—*two* years since Yvonne's death? God how I miss her.

Ladies and ladies, gentlemen and gentlemen, the pages are blank and the music has long been forgotten. The Widow Eleanor, aka Picasso, is still banging around the kitchen by the time her neighbors finally arrive. Mimi and that surly kid of hers—what's her name? *Violet*—are surprised to find the apartment free of clutter and grease and dust. Eleanor greets them in the foyer with a tentative smile.

Do I look like a clown? Eleanor asks, rather coyly. I hate when she stoops to fishing for compliments. The mongrel bitch knows perfectly well that she looks good. She's paid attention to her hygiene and taken the time to brush and pin up those long, silver tresses of hers. Ooh-la-la. Girlfriend's even thrown on an exquisite, moth-eaten caftan and put on red lipstick. A little smeared around the edges, but who gives a fuck? Chin up, shoulders back, tits and pelvis forward.

Mimi's never seen E so grand and femme. Dangling earrings of garnet and silver, rings and bangles of carnelian and turquoise, embroidered Moroccan slippers. Neo-hippie wardrobe and jewelry courtesy of the Museum of Yvonne.

You should wear that outfit to your reading at Volga, Mimi says, following Eleanor into the open kitchen. Very glam.

Eleanor glances at Mimi's bandaged arm. How's the arm doing?

Mimi gives a little shrug. Eleanor stirs her simmering curry with a wooden spoon. I may cancel, she murmurs.

Mimi stares at her in disbelief. What? Oh, no, Eleanor. You *can't.*

Oh, yes I can. I'm old. I can do anything.

You go, Eleanor. Violet giggles and heads straight for the sofa and the remote.

Project Runway's on, she announces gaily. Woo-hoo. Season finale!

Absolutely no TV tonight. I forbid it. Eleanor turns off the stove.

You're fucking kidding, right?

No, Violet. I'm fucking not, Eleanor says.

Mimi starts to say something, thinks better of it, and remains silent.

Pour us some, Eleanor says to Mimi, meaning the open bottle of white rioja on the counter. A bottle that is already half empty, mind you. To Violet, who is pouting, E says, Didn't forget about you, dear. There's plenty of Orangina in the fridge.

I prefer wine, the kid says.

Eleanor turns to Mimi. Do we have your permission?

Mimi shakes her head. School night, sorry.

Work lights from the construction site seep through the blinds in the living room. Those fucking lights are on all the time, Eleanor grumbles. Night and day, rain or shine.

Mimi looks out the window at the building. At least it's not another Richard Meier.

Natalie Portman and the Olsen twins are moving in, FYI. Violet's slumped down in a funk on the sofa.

Mimi makes a "no shit" face. Where'd you hear *that*?

Violet shrugs. Perez Hilton. Gawker. I dunno.

If Yvonne were alive, she'd put those twins in one of her paintings. I saw them this afternoon, says Eleanor.

Violet brightens. You did? Where?

On Bleecker, Eleanor answers. Spooky little things, they are.

The ladies take their place at the table, which is covered with a dazzling *ikat* fabric woven by land-mine amputees in Siem Reap, Cambodia. Eleanor's outdone herself. Candles, a vase of perky daffodils, little jars of various condiments. Mimi's baffled by all the fuss, Violet profoundly bored. The kid's laying it on real thick, still furious about missing her season finale. A giddy Eleanor dishes out hearty servings of prawn curry and saffron rice, ignoring Violet's *Just a little, please,* bit of admonition. Eleanor does a sloppy job, spilling sauce on the silk tablecloth. Oops, she murmurs. Eleanor looks down at her hand, then around the room.

Maybe sensing a presence, maybe not. She raises her wineglass in a toast. To beautiful food. And beautiful neighbors. Even the kid has to smile. To Beauty, Violet says, raising her glass of Orangina. And the Beast! For a brief instant, death is nothing but a tantalizing whore with a knife in her hand. For a brief instant, everyone is happy and content.

Mimi realizes she's famished and digs in to the fiery curry. Poor Mimi. She grabs her water glass and starts drinking.

I used those deadly little peppers. Can't take it? Eleanor asks.

Guess not. Mimi pours herself more water.

Water only makes it worse, Eleanor says. She turns to Violet. Are you on some kind of diet? You haven't touched your food.

I'm in mourning, Violet answers. Great Beasty is dead.

Of course. I understand. Maybe you can have a little dessert when we're done, Eleanor says. I made rice pudding with cardamom from scratch.

No thank you, says Violet.

Tonight is almost too easy, but I'm having fun. What a delicious disaster. Eleanor keeps glancing at the door, like some trembling ingenue waiting for her first love. Praying that Benjy and Nneka will surprise us all by showing up. Fool. The pages are blank, the music long forgotten. Would you believe the way Bolaño's being fetishized? Eleanor says to no one in particular. He must be laughing in his grave.

Who's Bolaño? Violet yawns. Mimi thinking of a polite way to exit. The pizzeria run by the Pakistanis delivers until midnight. Their pizzas are gooey and salty, just what she and Violet crave.

And that VH1 tribute to Romeo Byron was on again today, E continues, oblivious. Did you catch it? Bunch of crap. Interviews with people who didn't even know him. Everyone lying through their teeth!

Sucks, mumbles Violet.

Sucks indeed, Eleanor mutters.

I had no idea you were such a fan. Mimi's face is flushed; she's on her way to being drunk. Never mind the shitty food, the weird atmosphere, the fact that her lips and tongue are burning. Happy drunk makes up for all of it. Mimi reaches for another bottle of rioja—*You mind, Eleanor?*— and opens it. Refills Eleanor's glass and hers. Violet frowning.

Mimi raises her glass of wine. To Romeo!

To the dead, Eleanor says. She drinks, eyes fixed on the door.

Are you expecting more people? Mimi asks her.

Hell no.

Violet turns to her mother in frustration. Can I go? School tomorrow—remember?

You can't leave yet, Eleanor interjects before Mimi can answer. I need two sets of eyes to help me find a painting.

Mom.

I'll stay and help Eleanor. You go on home, Mimi says, trying to appease Violet. She is not too drunk to miss the implication of the word *home.* Whose home, et cetera.

Why can't you come with me?

I won't be long. Good night, Violet.

Violet slams the door when she leaves.

Your kid's a royal pain in the ass, Eleanor says.

Mimi unmoved. Yeah, so . . . We gonna look for this fucking painting, or WHAT?

They get down on their hands and knees and look under and behind the sofa, the desk in the study, Eleanor's bed. Mimi pulls aside the shower curtain. The painting of the jaguar/woman made her heart stop the first time she saw it. Dark, smeared, hauntingly familiar. Mouth wide open, ready to swallow the world.

You sure you didn't sell or give it away? Mimi asks, sober by now. They are back in the living room. Eleanor's long white hair has come undone. She looks ancient and ravaged, more beautiful than ever.

No, Eleanor says. I would never do that.

Mimi takes a deep breath. That painting was, like, the size of a wall. It can't just *disappear.*

Yvonne hid it. Don't you see?

You're giving me the creeps.

Eleanor chuckles. That's ironic, coming from you.

Mimi gets on her feet. I'm going home. You should get some sleep. You look like you haven't slept in ages.

Sleep's for the young. Eleanor reaches into the pocket of her caftan and pulls out a vial. She unscrews the cap/spoon, aware that Mimi is watching her intently. The lost pages, the forgotten music, the dead silence.

They were at it for a while. Three in the morning, maybe later. Picasso outdid herself, Picasso splurged. So what if the old girl's mind is gone and she can't cook anymore? Mimi thinks. I've achieved a raggedy nirvana, a fleeting bliss.

Eleanor?

Yes, dear.

I'm broke.

Which means?

Can't get my movie made.

Finished your script?

Well—

All about money, huh.

Always.

Bullshit.

What do you mean, bullshit?

Your first movie was made on the fly, with a lovely cast of amateurs and very little money. Why not do it the same way again?

Mimi tries not to tremble from all the coke. The way it came together was a miracle. I didn't know what I was doing.

My wings flutter. Eleanor feels something brush against her skin and slither out of the shadowy room. She wants desperately to follow but crawls over to the credenza instead. What are you doing? Mimi asks in a wan, dejected voice. Eleanor combs through her library of DVDs until she finds *Blood Wedding.* It's about time you saw this again, kiddo.

Blood Wedding

Casting the movie had been a hoot. A blast, a goof. The only professional hired was a ghostly, fifty-something-year-old tweaker named Irene Sykes. Her résumé was impressive, though badly in need of updating. There had been a recurring role as a judge on *Law & Order* back in the nineties. Bit parts on gritty HBO dramas. *Oz. The Wire.* Irene had even made a killing as the voice of the queen bee in an animated national commercial for Feminex, a drug used to control bladder leakage in women. *Side effects may include: headache, nausea, vomiting, diarrhea, dry mouth, panic, anxiety, and abnormal dreams.* Desperate Irene had burned some bridges and was willing to work for scale with a first-time director. Mimi couldn't believe her luck. Against everyone's advice, she cast Irene as the bride's vengeful mother. Mimi believed that attention, flattery, and encouragement were all that Irene Sykes needed in order to deliver. Her strategy worked. Irene's memorably bizarre performance was cited by discerning critics and fans of shock and gore. Mimi's secret nickname for her: Irene Yikes.

A blast, a goof. Bobby agreed to play the groom. It was a nonspeaking part; all Bobby had to do was stand there and look pretty. And after weeks of dispiriting auditions with perky blondes fresh out of drama school, Mimi decided to cast the unknown and untried Darlene Drayton (born Perpetua Cienfuegos in El Paso, Texas) in the starring role of the bride. She was a stripper friend of Bobby's, lovingly described as an amazon goddess with charisma, brains, and perfect boobs. *Big, but not too big. Firm, but not too firm. None of that implant shit, know what I'm sayin'? Darlene gives you real.*

A blast, a goof. The story of Perpetua/Darlene got juicier every time Bobby told it. Mimi was sufficiently hooked to keep listening. Darlene was a distant cousin of Bobby's, some sort of business associate from the old days. Running shit across borders and continents on Bobby's behalf, living a thousand lives. High-school dropout, runaway, autodidact, reformed crackhead, yoga devotee, voracious reader of poetry. Some of Darlene's favorite poems: "Somnambulant Ballad." "Monologue of a Dog Ensnared in History." "You Bring Out the Mexican in Me."

She had done time and deserved a medal for what she'd been through. But most of all, Bobby said, Darlene deserved a medal for being a heroic single mom to little Isis.

A stab of jealousy. A cigarette. Mimi bursts out laughing.

Oh. My. God.

What.

The way you're talking.

What.

You've never gotten over it.

What.

Saint Darlene.

Bobby's smile was cagey. Want her in your movie or what?

I dunno, Bobby. Can the bitch act? The kid yours?

He kept smiling. She could not read his face.

The more cautious and sober members of Mimi's production team grew worried, detecting faint whiffs of destruction in the air. But Mimi was not to be stopped. She was determined to meet and audition Darlene.

Boomerang was a so-called gentlemen's club out by Newark Airport.

The club's flashy Web site boasted VIP amenities, full bottle service, prime rib, and the most beautiful exotic entertainers in the world. Darlene was in the middle of her act when Mimi and Bobby walked in on a Saturday night. Every seat was taken, so they headed straight for the bar. Bobby had a little chat with the cheerful topless bartender, who seemed to be fond of him. Two generous doubles of Cuervo Gold suddenly appeared. Mimi made sure to sip hers.

The topless girls had it down to a science, managing to stay out of harm's way as they doled out platters of lukewarm nachos and four-hundred-dollar buckets of Smirnoff to the tense, horny men in the audience. All eyes fixed on the fierce, intimidating woman dancing before them, naked except for her high-heeled patent-leather boots and the tiniest of G-strings. A husky male voice crackling with anger and desire rapped on the sound track. *Pussy. Fame. Money. Betrayal. Vengeance. Death.* The rhymes were hokey and uninspired, but it didn't matter. The men grew quiet as Darlene caressed herself in a hot, white circle of light and gyrated slowly to the pulsing, ominous groove.

Mimi, who was the only woman in the room with all her clothes on, stood close to Bobby. They had done a few lines in his Camaro before going inside the club; Mimi was feeling antsy and vulnerable. She was definitely turned on by what was happening onstage, but also profoundly detached. Like she was already dead. Bobby, on the other hand, was in his element and could not shut up. He ordered another round, without bothering to ask if she wanted it. Darlene's been taking acting lessons with this guy, Stein. Guy's old and doesn't take just anybody. Works with all the cool people. Ethan Hawke. Marisa Tomei. Romeo Byron. That fat dude who won the Oscar—what's his name? Bobby waited for Mimi to provide him with the answer, but she was distracted by Darlene's lewd interpretation of a yoga scorpion pose. The audience went wild.

They drank and watched Darlene do her thing, watched the audience make fools of themselves. Darlene was *hot,* Bobby cocky and proud, clapping and whistling when Darlene's set was over, a stab of jealousy, Mimi thinking she was in love with Bobby and could that ever work?

Are we going backstage? Mimi asked him.

The bouncer with the shaved head was right out of central casting. Big, buff, probably on steroids, and just back from Iraq, ready to protect Darlene Drayton from the hammered frat boys and melancholy stalkers who might be lurking in the shadows. Except nothing was happening, and he was bored. At the sight of Bobby, he perked up. 'Sup, man? Long time no see. Bobby didn't bother introducing Mimi and whispered something in the bouncer's ear instead, making him laugh. The bouncer pulled aside the dusty black velvet curtain to let them through. Backstage at Boomerang was a bleak affair. She's the only one with her own dressing room, Bobby said as he knocked softly on Darlene's door. They were happy to see each other. You could tell by the way Darlene's face lit up and Bobby's, too. Mimi felt another pang, but Darlene was quick and held out her hand. You must be Bobby's friend the *filmmaker,* Darlene said. Not like she was making fun of Mimi, but with a warm smile. Bobby said just enough about the movie to stoke Darlene's interest even more, then left for the parking lot with the bouncer. Who wanted to check out Bobby's restored '98 Camaro, maybe do a little blow. Get twisted.

The women compared snapshots of their daughters. She's an old soul, Darlene said, studying Violet's somber class photo. Who doesn't like me very much, Mimi said. Typical mother-daughter shit, Darlene said. It'll pass. What sign are you? Scorpio with Gemini rising. For real? So am I. Sweet, Mimi said. I'll do your movie for no money if you like my audition, Darlene said. Meeting you is a sign. Your movie is a sign. I believe in signs.

Word, Mimi said. Whatever Darlene needed to hear.

Bobby came back in a funny mood. He asked them if they wanted drinks, then offered to get them high, as much as they wanted, excellent rock from God-knows-where in Colombia or Bolivia, take it from me, ladies, you won't need very much. Mimi said yes to a drink—straight up Patrón, this time please, Bobby—and of course she said yes to more of his blow but tried to act cool around Darlene and not sound too eager. Darlene said no to everything. Since when? Bobby asked. Darlene rolled her eyes. Since the last time I told you. No shit, Bobby said. Darlene winked at Mimi. Gotta tell it like it is, girl. *The body is a temple.* And now that I'm a movie star . . .

~

In spite of all the lines they had done, Eleanor and Mimi kept nodding out. Mimi didn't mind the nod. She was sick of *Blood Wedding,* sick of Eleanor yammering about it like she always did. Though it was mad funny, she had to admit. How the two of them kept waking up at various intervals to the same damn opening scene, wondering if the disc was damaged or if they were stuck in a dream. The eerie sound track didn't help.

> *Sudden banging of piano keys, water dripping, a child crying softly in the distance. Alas, one of the few delights in this infuriating, delirious, often incomprehensible little horror film is the stunningly effective score composed by director Mimi Smith.*
>
> —Kevin Jamal Stokes, *SF Bay Guardian*

Not quite. There was never any money to hire a real composer, so with the help of GarageBand, Sounddogs.com, and her Mac, Mimi was forced to become one. Carmelo was surprised when Mimi called, asking if she could come over to record him. *Doing what?* Cecil Taylor meets Chopin. I need you to mix it up and freak 'em out, Mimi said. Carmelo laughed. Then he told her to fuck off and leave him alone. He hated the idea of Mimi showing up at his apartment with some

DJ/audio engineer/one-night stand of hers in tow. He had not played in years, and the piano he owned was nothing but an upright piece of shit. Mimi cajoled, cursed, and pleaded until Carmelo finally broke down and agreed. It took all night, a lot of blow, and what seemed like hundreds of takes, but the music he came up with was perfect. Ominous, spare, tinged with sorrow. Carmelo refused to be acknowledged for his contribution and asked that his name not appear in the credits. Mimi remembers hearing him grunt as he played. A long-overdue elegy for their murdered parents was buried somewhere in those deep, dark chords. She believes it to this day.

The bride plucks her own eyes out and doesn't scream. She drops her eyeballs on a small silver platter and takes the platter with her as she begins her climb. Tracking shot as the bride ascends the steep, winding staircase of an empty house. Her wedding gown is splattered with blood. Her face. Water slowly drips and segues into steady rainfall, then into a choir of chanting female voices (referred to in Mimi's script as "a choir of blind, grieving mothers"). The gibberish they chant sounds vaguely like Latin. The bride with no eyes is guided up the stairs by some inner force. She never stumbles, turning corners without pause or complaint. A shadowy figure waits at the top of the stairs. The camera zooms in—

Mimi used the remote to turn the movie off and tried to remain calm. Her sinuses and lungs were clogged. She was forced to breathe through her mouth. The sudden silence woke Eleanor. What happened? Where's Violet? Did we find it?

Violet went home hours ago. And no, we didn't find it. Mimi stretched her arms and got off the sofa. I should go. Violet will be up soon.

Wanna pick me up?

That coke's garbage. I truly worry about you, Mimi said.

You worry about *me*? Don't blame the product, little girl. Admit you pigged out, like you always do.

I'm dying here. My nose—

Eleanor was not impressed. There's Afrin in the bathroom. Help yourself.

The medicine cabinet was a cokehead's dream. Mimi was amused to find more than one kind of Afrin. Original, Severe Congestion, Extra Moisturizing. She chose Severe Congestion, tilted her head back, and squirted it into her nostrils. The effect was miraculous. Next to the row of Afrin was a prescription bottle of Dilaudid made out to Yvonne Wilder. Expired but definitely still potent, Mimi thought. She jammed the pill bottle into her jeans pocket before sliding the cabinet door shut.

Eleanor was bent over the coffee table, scribbling in the kind of notebook Violet used in school. Fresh lines of white powder were laid out on a rectangular piece of glass. Mimi hesitated, then weakened and sat back down. In the middle of writing, Eleanor suddenly threw the pen aside and studied her right hand. Hideous, she muttered grimly. Fucking hideous. Eleanor picked up the glass straw and snorted a couple of lines. Her tone was brusque. Which books of mine have you read? Maybe none of them?

Eyes of a Jaguar.

How'd you manage to find it? It's been out of print for years.

Got it from an online reseller for fifty cents. Plus shipping and handling, Mimi couldn't resist adding.

Eleanor burst out laughing. *Fifty cents!*

Hardcover, in mint condition. I'll give it to you.

It's not very good. I don't want it.

How can you say that? It's your work.

Precisely, Eleanor said. A long, uncomfortable moment passed in which Eleanor stared with longing at Mimi. Finally Eleanor spoke. How much do you need to make your next movie?

Mimi did a fat line. You fucking with me, Eleanor?

I want to help you.

Because you wanna fuck me? I know you wanna fuck me.

If I were sober, we could argue about using the term *fuck,* but now's not the time. Do you find the idea of an old woman lusting after you repugnant? Grotesque?

You're high and lonely, Mimi said. This is all about Yvonne.

Don't tell me what this is about. Ever been with a woman? Eleanor took note of the faint blush spreading across Mimi's face. The bitch was clearly flattered.

This must be one of your standard pickup lines.

Keep stalling, Eleanor said.

Think I'm a whore?

Go ahead and be a whore if it excites you, but know this. I'll give you the money for your damn movie no matter what. That's how much I *love* you. Eleanor got on her knees and with surprising force spread Mimi's legs with her clawlike hands. She sniffed at Mimi's crotch, murmuring, Lovely, lovely, as she struggled to unzip Mimi's jeans. Mimi was horrified and aroused. It would've been easy to stop Eleanor from going any further, but she didn't. She glanced at the clock on the wall. Violet was probably awake.

You wet? Of course you're wet. Mimi closed her eyes as Eleanor began to lick her. The bottle of Dilaudid rolled across the floor. Eleanor was too busy to notice.

The Brother

He remembers the cemetery across the street. The house in Colma being small and boxy and hot. Behind the house was a patch of yard with a chain-link fence and a listless rottweiler who was slowly dying of boredom and neglect. The house and everything in it belonged to Evie; she never let anyone forget it. Evie was Uncle Frank's wife, a hefty blonde with a nasty laugh and glassy blue eyes. Frank adored her. On their way to pick up Carmelo and Mimi at the airport, Evie had asked Frank, So how long these relatives of yours planning to stay?

He remembers that he was seventeen and on his way to being fat, and that his sister had just turned fourteen when they arrived.

Carmelo and Mimi slept in the living room. Mimi on the sofa, Carmelo in a sleeping bag on the floor. Sometimes Ray-Ray and Lou, Evie's two sons from a previous marriage, would drop by to smoke pot and have a few beers with their mother on their way home from work. They acted like Frank didn't exist. Snickered at the strange music of his English, the way Frank pronounced words like *veh-jeh-tah-ball.* Ray-Ray and Lou, who'd both been in 'Nam, were overly friendly with Mimi. Carmelo was afraid of them. He and Mimi couldn't wait to escape.

The ocean is a mother. Carmelo remembers learning how to surf in Santa Cruz. Going back to the sad, boxy little house in Colma so he could stuff his face and dream at night about his parents. In one dream his mother laughs as she chases a cloud rat around the garden of their old house. A pink satin ribbon is tied around the cloud rat's neck. In another dream his father clutches a brown paper lunch bag while he walks through a dense alpine forest. In a small clearing, his father looks around to make sure no one is following, then opens the bag and dumps out hundreds of eyes onto the hard, snowy ground.

Carmelo surveys the living room. The stacks of magazines and newspapers have grown higher. Labyrinths of headlines and bylines, alluring images, fonts of rage. There is still time to save the planet and himself. He could bundle everything up, leave it all on the sidewalk. Bundles of paper, bundles of trees. Clean house. What was it his sponsor used to say? *A clean house shall set you free.* And yet. The yearning. The sponsor wasn't very helpful when it came to that. Carmelo had been good. There was nothing in the apartment—no drink, no smoke, no nothing. It was easy enough to make a trip to the liquor store down the block, the one with the bulletproof window. Or call his ex-wife, Brenda. Brenda would calm him down. Brenda was a woman of faith, an optimist and a striver. Not one of Carmelo's usual fluttery, vapid *girls.* She had worked around food all her life; she was not afraid of knives and believed in heaven. They met at an Al-Anon meeting. Carmelo was not the testifying or confessional type; he did not crave attention. He had gone to the meeting out of guilt and desperation, wanting maybe to talk about the burden of being an older brother. Mimi's enabler. Carmelo liked the word *enabler.* It was new to him and sounded just about right. The meetings were held on Wednesday evenings, in the dreary parish hall of a Catholic church on the far end of Christopher Street. Carmelo got there early and hovered by the doorway. A children's tap-dance class had just ended. The large, fluorescent-lit room was bustling with harried women and sweaty, exuberant kids anxious to get home. A sturdy, cheerful-looking young woman entered and began arranging folding chairs in a semicircle. Followed by a tattooed old man with a limp, who was trying his best to help her. The young woman noticed Carmelo. *You here for the meeting?* Carmelo nodded. Welcome, she said. My name is Brenda. And this is Thomas. Wanna help us set up?

~

Why do you come to these things?

I don't have to answer that.

If a guy like *me* can share, then *you* can share.

Sharing's a good thing.

——

You should feel good about what happened tonight.

I shouldn't've said what I said. Don't like talkin' about . . . you know. Private stuff.

It's not easy.

How come *you* didn't talk?

No one has to. Listening can be just as useful.

Yeah, right.

You're coming back, I hope.

Why? Think I'm cute?

Grow up.

Sorry. I didn't mean—

Whatever, Carmelo. It's Carmelo, right?

You bet. But you can call me Melo.

You believe in God?

Sometimes.

I come to these meetings because of Jane, my sister. She's clean now, but—

Your sister. My sister. That's heavy.

Brenda rolled her eyes. Like I said. Grow up, Melo.

~

Usually he got her voice mail. Brenda never answered her cell when she was driving that Volvo of hers, which seemed to be every minute of every waking hour now that she lived in Los Angeles. But today was different. Hey, Melo, Brenda greeted him warmly. How goes it? Carmelo had not spoken to her in at least a year. I can't believe it, he said. Can't believe what? She kept up the casual, friendly tone. It was noon in her part of the world. You answering the phone. She was silent, so he tried again. Getting ready for the lunch crowd? Last he'd heard, Brenda and her sister Jane had opened a seafood-and-steak house across from the Marina del Rey Yacht Club. I'm actually home, still in my pajamas, Brenda said. We sold the business. No kidding, Carmelo said. Thought you were doing really well. We were. But everyone was stealing from us. The manager, the bartender, a couple of waiters. Brenda groaned in mock despair. That's too bad, Carmelo said. You okay? Of course I'm okay, Brenda retorted. Busy finding investors for something new, as a matter of fact. I want to open a dumpling-and-noodle bar. Her tone darkened. You in trouble, Melo?

Nope.

Please don't lie to me.

I'm not.

Need to borrow money or what?

A cousin of mine's missing. We think she's been murdered.

Gee whiz. That's *awful.* Is there something I can do to help?

Don't hang up on me, whatever you do.

I won't.

Promise?

Melo, for godsake. After a pause Brenda said, You still going to meetings, I hope. And *church.* And keeping up with the piano. She was a firm believer in rehab and redemption. And the arts.

Had a little relapse earlier this year, but—

What kind of relapse?

No big deal. I'm back on track.

That's terrific. You can do it, Melo. I know you can.

He imagined her sprawled on some Pottery Barn couch in her cutesy pajamas, a worried frown on her face. You working? Brenda suddenly asked. You're too old and too smart to keep living like— Brenda stopped herself. She did not want to hurt him. Well, anyway. That job you have at the— Where is it again?

Brooklyn Museum. Security guard. No longer relevant.

Oh, God. You quit.

I miss you, Brenda.

No.

You're the best thing that ever—

We can't go there. Brenda's voice grew sharp.

Carmelo knew he was blowing it, but the neediness kept spilling out of him. You seeing anyone? It's okay, you can be honest, I'm cool with it.

Sorry about your cousin.

I love you, Brenda.

I will always be your friend. Whatever you need. I mean it.

Her kindness stabbed him like a knife. I don't want to be your friend.

Brenda sighed. I pray for you, Melo. All the time.

~

Their marriage had lasted eighteen months. Carmelo remained sober and clean throughout. He went to church with Brenda and grew thick eating her food. There were those moments. Carmelo would become restless, hang out with Mimi and Bobby and binge. Brenda always knew when Carmelo slipped, but she didn't call him on it. She watched and waited. One day while Carmelo was out, she packed what was important to her and left. Just like that. Scribbled a terse little note and taped it on the piano. *I'm filing for a divorce. Moving back to L.A. Don't follow me.* Carmelo laughed when he read it, thinking it was another one of her pranks. He called Trattoria Barzini and asked for her. I'm sorry, but she no longer works here, the manager said. Tell Brenda it's her husband calling, Carmelo said, still in a jovial mood. Thinking, They're all in on the prank. The manager spoke in a gentler tone. I'm sorry, but . . . Brenda quit two weeks ago. She said there was a family emergency.

In a zombie state, Carmelo walked all the way downtown. It took him close to three hours. Bobby buzzed him into Mimi's apartment.

Wazzup man? Long time no see.

She left me, Carmelo mumbled.

No shit? Bobby wasn't surprised. Brenda was a ballbuster.

Where's my sister?

Upstate. I'm supposed to go up there this weekend. This acting shit's a lotta work. She wants to reshoot one of my scenes. Wanna come? I'm takin' my ride.

I wanna get high.

C'mon, man. You don't mean that.

Carmelo looked at him.

Carmelo followed Bobby into the living room and sat down on the sofa. He closed his eyes. You okay, man? Bobby asked. Carmelo opened his eyes and didn't answer. Bobby poured them each a glass of Maker's Mark. They sipped the bourbon in silence. Bobby left the room and came back with a vial of cocaine. He laid out a neat row of lines on the coffee table with his credit card. Carmelo rolled up a twenty-dollar bill and gave Bobby a melancholy smile. Go ahead, my friend, Bobby said.

ART · ARCHITECTURE · LITERATURE · FILM · PERFORMANCE · VOLGABLOG

the Volga Review

*Fifth Anniversary * Special Issue*

ELEANOR DELACROIX: PORTFOLIO & INTERVIEW

Excerpts from Delacroix's 2001 memoir, California Melancholy

Handbags

My mother's addiction to Benzedrine and gin was no secret in our house. She was also a handbag junkie and had quite a collection—Lucite buckets, beaded clutches, bamboo birdcages, rattan picnic hampers. Whenever in distress, which was often—Mom would run out and buy more. Poor Ann (Ana Rosario Vargas on her birth certificate) was oblivious to the fact that everyone in the family had, at some point, come across the Bennie inhaler and little silver flask stashed away in that alligator handbag of hers. We all pretended that it was perfectly normal. When I was nine, I filched her inhaler and stayed awake for three days. My secret.

The Wizard of Oz

But where in Sacramento could Mom go to buy Lucite buckets studded with rhinestones? Did she have to put on a hat and little white gloves and drive all the way to San Francisco? Did she prefer Gump's over City of Paris over I. Magnin? Did my father approve? Was I forced to put on a Sunday frock and act as her little chaperone on these excursions? Did we have tea and crumpets at Blum's? What year are we talking about? What kind of car did my mother—I mean *Ana Rosario*—drive? Was she a reckless driver? Did I listen to the radio and daydream while she drove? "Over the Rainbow"? "Strange Fruit"? Who was marching into Poland while I daydreamed? Did Ana smoke Kents or Chesterfields while driving? Did my father approve? Why did Ana forbid me to call San Francisco "Frisco"? Did she actually say it made me sound like a sailor? Was I with her when she picked up that sailor in Union Square? Was I with her when she took him to the Clift Hotel? Did she slip me money and send me off to see *The Wizard of Oz* by myself? Did a man move down next to me in the dark theater and rest his clammy hand on my thigh? Did I let him slowly pull up my skirt? Did I hold my breath? Close my eyes? How many times did I sit through the movie?

The War

Two of my brothers were killed. Another—a survivor of the Bataan Death March—went crazy.

Jealousy

I ended up being fucked by Jocanda Fox in more ways than you can imagine. Completely destroyed, but wanting more. Jocanda was quite open about her long-standing relationship with the infamous, cross-dressing bolero singer Magda Beltrán. She bragged about being Magda's main paramour quite often, as a matter of fact. Jocanda enjoyed making me jealous. I soon discovered that jealousy made for great sex.

"Noche de Amor." "María Linda." "Alma de Mujer" (supposedly written for Jocanda). "La Gitana." And there was that other song, "Lágrimas Negras," which Magda didn't write but turned into a big crossover hit. I remember hearing it on the radio and wishing her dead.

The Mexicans revered Magda Beltrán. Her tragic boleros and distinctive, sandpaper voice moved them in profound and mysterious ways. Magda broke all the rules. She was ugly but sexy, carried a switchblade, was fond of guns, cursed, drank, smoked Cuban cigars, seduced married women, and dared to write songs about her conquests. Magda Beltrán's carefully constructed image was of a dangerous dyke cowboy, albeit one with a noticeable limp. Compared to her I was nothing but a bore. Little Mary Sunshine from Sacramento. College girl. Earnest, pallid, provincial. A bore.

Taboo

I was home for the holidays when I decided to announce that I was in love with a woman. The war was over. My parents went about their business with their jaws clenched, incandescent with grief. Quietly drunk and buzzed by five in the afternoon. Only one son left who was sane and alive. And *he* was out of the house, living in another state with his own secrets. And then? There was the daughter. Me. A puzzle. My affair with Jocanda Fox—illicit, taboo, exciting—made me feel strangely powerful. I was high on sex, high on loving women and myself, indestructible. Either too dumb or too defiant to keep my mouth shut.

It was a tense, silent dinner at the kitchen table, just the three of us. Mashed potatoes, roast chicken, boiled string beans. I'm in love, I blurted out. What? my father said. His face was flushed from scotch and sodas. What? my mother said. I'm in love with my professor, I said. My mother stared at me. What? my father said. You met her when you and Mom visited Mills, I said. I couldn't help smiling, which made things worse. *Her?* my father said. Professor Fox, I said. Professor Jocanda Fox.

It all happened very fast. My father stood up, came around the table, and punched me. I remember spitting out a bloody tooth. Maybe two. My father shook with rage. He threatened to have me lobotomized. Threatened to call Mills and have That Mexican Whore fired. Threatened to call the cops and have That Mexican Whore arrested and deported. That Mexican Whore, he kept muttering. Ann—my mestiza mother with the anglicized name—sat frozen in her chair and stared at me.

Refuge

Aunt Elly took me in. Elly who had never married and lived alone and feared no one. She listened quietly when I told her about Jocanda. Have I scandalized you? I remember asking my aunt. No, Elly said. Why not? I asked. I seem to remember being slightly miffed. Why not why not? Elly laughed.

She gave me money and took me to the bus station. I remember trying not to cry as we said our good-byes. I sat in the waiting area for hours, paralyzed by indecision. *Where should I go? What should I do?* A cop wandered over and asked if I was planning on spending the night. He said it with a smile, but I knew what he was implying. I got off that bench and bought a one-way ticket to New York City. I'd read the books. I'd seen the movies. I wanted to be a writer. According to Peter Hawthorne—he was no longer Pop, Papa, Daddy, *my father,* just Peter Hawthorne—I was a pervert who needed to be lobotomized. There were plenty of unlobotomized, pervert writers in New York City. I'd learned that at Mills, from Jocanda Fox.

Flaming Horses

My parents were both killed in a car accident in 1962. They were on their way to Del Mar. Some guy driving a truck towing a trailer with two Arabian mares lost control. Jumped the median and crashed into my father's Plymouth. Everything burst into flames. I was going to add "including the horses," but I won't. Aunt Elly sent me the rather lengthy obituary notice published in the *Sacramento Bee.* Needless to say, I was not invited to the funeral.

the INTERVIEW

Delacroix was born Mary Hawthorne eighty years ago in Sacramento, California. She was the only girl and the youngest of five children—referred to as W, X, Y, and Z in her memoir, *California Melancholy*—born to Peter Hawthorne and Ann Vargas. The family was prosperous, staunchly Catholic, well respected. Delacroix's father was a prominent lawyer, active in local politics. He once ran for mayor of Sacramento and almost won. Delacroix's mother was a former Miss Sacramento.

Delacroix went to Mills, then an all-women liberal-arts college in Oakland, California. The experience changed her life in more ways than one. In her final undergraduate year, Delacroix became sexually involved with literary scholar and translator Jocanda Fox, a visiting professor of Romance languages and literature from Mexico. Fox, who was fifteen years older than Delacroix, initiated the intense affair.

Little Deaths, Delacroix's first book of fiction, tells the shocking story of a torrid love affair between a headstrong fifteen-year-old girl and her magnetic forty-five-year-old tutor, an ex-nun. The relationship culminates in a brutal murder. Delacroix was thirty-seven years old when the ninety-page novella was bought by Moss Blake, then editor in chief of Left Bank.

The novel catapulted the press- and camera-shy author into the spotlight and international fame. A letter for her from Jocanda Fox arrived at the editorial offices of Left Bank.

In it, Fox expressed admiration for Delacroix's novel and remorse about the way she had treated her former student. ("Mary/Eleanor: You were lovely and open and curious. I was monstrous and careless with your love, thinking only of myself.") Fox informed Delacroix that Magda Beltrán was dead, shot while performing one of her sold-out concerts in Mexico City. The killer turned out to be the humiliated husband of a woman with whom Beltrán was having an affair. ("A fitting end for Magda, don't you think?") Fox then asked for permission to do the Spanish translation of *Little Deaths*. ("I will understand if you say no.") Delacroix took almost a year to respond but finally gave her blessing. The two began corresponding regularly.

In the United States, an attempt to ban *Little Deaths* as obscene made headlines but was thrown out of the courts (see *Howl*, *People v. Ferlinghetti*, and *Tropic of Cancer*, *Miller v. California*). Delacroix kept declining requests for interviews and photos. Because of her sudden notoriety, she was forced to move from her tiny Greenwich Village walk-up and into the guest bedroom of the Upper West Side apartment Moss Blake shared with architect Philip Gottlieb, Blake's partner at the time. The setup was temporary, as Gottlieb and Delacroix didn't get along.

Tired of being "homeless" and anxious to start a new novel, Delacroix accepted an invitation from Fox to come to Mexico City and stay for as long as she liked in the palatial family home Jocanda shared with her twin sister, Guadalupe. Guadalupe was a prominent art collector and historian, rumored to have been the lover of both Diego Rivera and Frida Kahlo. Delacroix lived in a guest cottage (Casita Verde) on the Fox property for six years. It was a productive time for her. She wrote two novels in quick succession, *Onyx* and *Eyes of a Jaguar*, also published by Left Bank. When Left Bank was sold to the Sandhaus conglomerate and promptly dismantled, Moss Blake resigned and started his own literary agency. Delacroix asked him to represent her.

Blake remained Delacroix's loyal agent, champion, and confidant until his death in 2002.

Our conversation took place in Manhattan's Meatpacking District over the course of two evenings in the apartment Delacroix shared with painter Yvonne Wilder until Wilder's death in 2007. The apartment was spacious, chaotic, and oddly elegant, with polished wood floors, high ceilings, shelves of books, and Day of the Dead figurines collected by Wilder and Delacroix over the years. Of course there were paintings and framed drawings by Wilder and other artists of distinction on the walls, including an early acrylic-and-paper collage by a then-unknown Jean-Michel Basquiat. ("He only wanted two hundred bucks," Delacroix said to us. "Yvonne gave him a bit more. He was—shall we say—rather desperate at the time.")

In the windowless study, described by Delacroix as "in a perpetual state of disorder," there was a wall devoted to photographs. Wilder with her son, Benjamin. Lupe and Jocanda Fox with their dogs. Felix Montoya and Delacroix. Moss Blake with Delacroix and James Baldwin. Manuel Puig with Paloma Picasso and her ex-husband and business partner, Rafael Lopez-Cambil. A grinning and bedraggled-looking Basquiat. An unknown Asian woman.

A striking woman with slate-gray eyes and long white hair, Delacroix greeted us at the door in bare feet. She wore a beautiful, faded caftan embroidered with tiny mirrors. We sat down for the interview in her living room. We were offered a choice of tequila or gin and tonics, which we declined, and served tasty olive and goat-cheese tarts, which Delacroix had made herself that morning. Although she looked younger than her eighty years and was in a curiously chatty and convivial mood, Delacroix complained of a chronic sinus condition and painful, debilitating arthritis in her hands. She declined to be photographed for this article.

—Sasha Collins and Rajiv Gill, 2009

VOLGA REVIEW

After a lifetime of saying no to interviews, why did you finally say yes?

ELEANOR DELACROIX

I have no idea. I do enjoy that scrappy little journal of yours, but this may end up being one of the dumbest things I've ever done.

VR

We are absolutely honored and thrilled to be here.

DELACROIX

Good for you.

VR

Tell us about your nom de plume.

DELACROIX

An homage to my Aunt Eleanor. My father's sister. One tough cookie, incredibly smart and outspoken. Blamed the Catholic Church for most of the world's ills. I loved how she doted on me and always stood up to my father.

VR

Does "Delacroix" have anything to do with the painter?

DELACROIX

I chose it because the two names sound good together. That's all.

VR

Your last work of fiction, *Savage Appetites,* was published by Sandhaus back in 1990. It's been nineteen years of silence since then. Have you made a conscious decision to stop writing novels?

DELACROIX

I've made a conscious decision that it's fucking okay not to be as prolific as some of my contemporaries. I've always been a slow writer. The older I get, the more agonizing it becomes. It's all in the revisions, as I used to say over and over again to my poor students. So what if you think you're brilliant? You have to try it again. Play around with the goddamn sentence like a painting. Hang it upside down, sideways, set the edges on fire. So maybe you end up going back to what you had originally, since that initial raw purge is usually the best. But so what? At least you might come to some sort of understanding. Of what works and why, that sort of thing.

VR

Sounds like torture.

DELACROIX

Writing is.

VR

Does it always have to be torture for it to be any good?

DELACROIX

I find the word *torture* sorely lacking. Nowadays all it brings to mind are unfortunate men standing on crates with sacks thrown over their heads. I prefer to think of writing as exquisite agony. Chalk it up to the Catholic in me, which—no matter how much I try—I can't seem to shake.

VR

Not many people know you've taught.

DELACROIX

In Mexico. Cambodia. Never in this country.

VR

Is that true? We heard you once taught at Smith. And at Columbia.

DELACROIX

I'm not the sort of writer in fashion with current M.F.A. creative-writing programs, if that's what you mean. First of all, I'm too fucking old. Yvonne and I—we were invited to lead workshops with women in Cambodia who had witnessed and experienced awful things during the reign of Pol Pot. Awful, awful things. So fucking awful that many of the women had gone blind.

VR

Hysterical blindness?

DELACROIX

That's what some people call it. That word *hysteria* is an interesting one, isn't it? And so we went. The conditions at the women's center were pretty rough. I mean, these people had nothing. Most were illiterate, so . . . Yvonne and I brought suitcases filled with reams of paper, pencils and pens, charcoal sticks, sketch pads, watercolor sets, a tape recorder—whatever we thought might be useful. The women who were blind told or sang us their stories and dreams. The director of the center, a remarkable young Khmer woman named—shit! I can't remember her name!—acted as our translator. Yvonne and I were humbled the long difficult month we spent with these particular women. Their suffering was enormous. Incomprehensible. It still haunts me, you know. Our enterprise was such a profound failure.

VR

How?

DELACROIX

There we were, two well-educated, well-fed, well-intentioned foreigners—but in the end, what the fuck did we really accomplish? Were these impoverished, blind women any better off? I hardly think so.

VR

What about Mexico?

DELACROIX

That was certainly a much happier and more gratifying teaching experience.

VR

The National Autonomous University of Mexico, wasn't it? *(Delacroix nods.)* Did you teach in Spanish?

DELACROIX

My Spanish is a joke, but I tried. Thank God most of my students were fairly proficient in English. A lot of them were poets. Extremely well read. Extremely opinionated. Jocanda Fox was head of the department back then. She was responsible for my residency.

VR

Sarah Kirshner, in her book *Sapphic Divas,* wrote extensively about your relationship with Fox and calls it one of the most important and transformative friendships of your life. Do you agree?

DELACROIX

I was her student. She was my lover. What more can I say? Do you know I can revise one sentence, oh, maybe—

VR

Five or six times?

DELACROIX

More like twenty. At least twenty.

VR

That's what you told your students they had to do in order to be good writers?

(Delacroix laughs and doesn't answer.)

VR

The writer Felix Montoya was another close—

DELACROIX

I don't want to talk about Felix.

VR

Then can we talk about your first novel, *Little Deaths,* which is considered to be your masterpiece?

DELACROIX

My masterpiece. Cute.

VR

When it was published, *Little Deaths* was panned by Malcolm West in the *New York Times* as—

DELACROIX

"Pretentious filth masquerading as high art." Yup. I remember.

VR

West further dismissed you as "a perverse writer of modest talents." The book went on to become an international bestseller in spite of all the negative reviews. How did you withstand the criticism and controversy?

DELACROIX

The book's taboo subject matter was clearly the cause of much of the outrage, especially for a closeted old fart like West. I threw a party when that nasty son of a bitch died. I'm sure that my nonlinear narrative and juicy sexual descriptions didn't help matters at all. West and a lot of the old-guard American critics hated that kind of experimental work. Especially coming from a woman like me! I was not part of the eastern cultural establishment. I was a college dropout, a queer nobody from fucking Sacramento, California. But Rebecca Ballantine came to my defense in the *Evergreen Review.*

VR

Yes, we Googled it.

DELACROIX

Really? I sold my archives to the University of Texas and never bothered making copies of any of my clippings. The young don't know Rebecca Ballantine. Or anybody else I'm talking about, probably. Oh, how fabulous! I have a contentious relationship with my computer, but I love Google! Love Wikipedia!

VR

You're on Facebook.

DELACROIX

I beg your pardon?

VR

Someone started a fan club. Eight hundred and sixty people have signed on as fans of Eleanor Delacroix.

DELACROIX

That's insane.

(More laughter. Delacroix excuses herself to go to the bathroom and is gone for some time. She returns in a somewhat giddy, effusive mood. Delacroix pours herself a glass of tequila and lights up a Camel nonfilter.)

VR

What was your response to Ballantine's assertion that, in spite of all the hot sex in your first novel, the coolness of your prose and the underlying theme of murder brought to mind Alain Robbe-Grillet, Nathalie Sarraute, and other writers of the *nouveau roman* movement?

DELACROIX

I was flattered, but—*Nathalie Sarraute?* What a hoot. Rebecca was one of the few respected critics who took my novel seriously, though. So did Malcolm West's nemesis, that other closeted old fart, what's-his-name.

VR

Leonard Schilling.

DELACROIX

Leonard Schilling, oh, God yes. In *Playboy* magazine, of all places.

VR

We Googled him, too. Schilling called your novel "a landmark in avant-garde lesbian feminist erotic literature."

DELACROIX

Total bullshit. Schilling was always so busy trying to be hip he never made any sense. *Avant-garde lesbian feminist erotic?* Bring it on.

VR

But we like that he ended the article by saying, "Dirty books never go out of fashion, and *Little Deaths* is simply one of the dirtiest books ever written. Think of it as hot porn with brains. You won't feel embarrassed by reading it on the subway."

DELACROIX

After that piece came out, Hefner's people kept bugging Moss to have me do one of those interviews.

VR

You mean like—the official *Playboy* Interview?

DELACROIX

There was a time that a glorified titty magazine like *Playboy* was actually considered relevant. But of course I said no. I've made it a practice to say no to all interviews.

VR

Until this one.

DELACROIX

Exactly. So please get the fuck on with it. Are we going to talk about *Little Deaths* all night? It's not as if it's the only damn novel I've written that matters.

VR

No, of course not. But unlike your other novels, which have gone out of print, *Little Deaths* has endured and become a cult classic. It's been translated into at least twenty-seven languages and enjoys brisk sales to this day. What accounts for its lasting power?

DELACROIX

How should I know? I've been living off the proceeds of that book for forty years. It's not like I wrote any differently after that.

VR

Speaking of proceeds, the film rights to *Little Deaths* have been optioned over the years by a colorful assortment of international directors, producers, and film stars, yet never made. Louis Malle, Liliana Cavani, Jane Campion, Pedro Almodóvar—

DELACROIX

Ahh, Pedro. That would've been too perfect. Especially if he cast Penélope Cruz as the ex-nun.

VR

Aside from money in the bank, nothing has come of all this buzz and hype. Do you have any idea why?

DELACROIX

Darlin', it's a wonder any movie ever gets made.

VR

Since you're such a connoisseur, does it matter who ultimately ends up making the movie version of your book?

DELACROIX

Nope. But I've decided to give away the rights to a talented filmmaker who lives across the hall. You're familiar with the urban horror movie *Blood Wedding*?

VR

You mean your neighbor's Mimi—

DELACROIX

Don't you think she's got the right sensibility?

VR

What a brilliant idea.

DELACROIX

Can we move on?

VR

Let's talk about your memoir, *California Melancholy*.

DELACROIX

Which had the unfortunate distinction of being published the week of September 11, 2001. No one was interested in either reviewing or reading it.

VR

We were fortunate enough to have found a used copy at the Strand. *(Delacroix laughs.)* The memoir deals with growing up in Sacramento, going to Mills, and it ends with your early years in New York, working at a variety of jobs while trying to be a writer.

DELACROIX

Yup. Done it all. Proofreader, typist, fact-checker, salesgirl at Macy's and Woolworth's, drug dealer, assistant bartender at Cleo's Den. Either of you ever heard of Cleo's Den?

VR

It's mentioned in passing in Kirshner's book.

DELACROIX

Cleo's was one of the original Greenwich Village *dyke* bars. We had a great jukebox and hosted the occasional drunken poetry reading. But then Cleo's got raided, and that was that. End of an era.

VR

Were you thrown in jail?

DELACROIX

Lucky for me, it was my night off. . . . But Cleo and everyone else got hauled away.

VR

Can you tell us about being a drug dealer?

DELACROIX

Why?

VR

Women dealing drugs—that's unusual.

DELACROIX

I didn't do it for long. People going in and out of my apartment at all hours of the day and night—not my cup of tea! You try to stay under the radar, keep your clientele small and exclusive, but hubris and greed tend to get in the way.

VR

What kind of drugs did you—

DELACROIX

Wanna hear about this memoir or what?

VR

Yes, we do.

DELACROIX

My original idea was to write a trilogy. The second book was going to be much longer and less grim than all that family drama. I wanted to explore those years in Mexico. The third would be about life with Yvonne back in New York. But then Moss died.

VR

Moss Blake.

DELACROIX

That's right. Moss had arranged for the memoirs to be published by Electra Press in London. I was no longer a sought-after writer, but Electra was a perfectly respectable, independent press. Run by women, so I was pleased. When Part One of the memoir came out after 9/11 and did so poorly . . . well, who can blame anyone? It was bad timing. When Moss died, there was no one left to push the second book forward and then . . . well. And then.

VR

Electra Press folded.

DELACROIX

Everyone was dying or dead or getting sick around me. I did not feel motivated to write those second and third books. The irony is, those books would've been fun. My life hasn't been just one big tragic soap opera, you know. There were incredible times, filled with incredible, beautiful, smart, and sexy people who were *fun*. Very entertaining to read about.

VR

Starting with the Fox twins?

DELACROIX

Absolutely, yes. Lupe had the most amazing art collection. And these hairless Aztec dogs who followed me around the garden. *Xoloitzcuintle.* Lupe and Jocanda called them "kwink-klez" for short. There was an ugly mama dog and two male pups. Freaky little beasts, they were—black and squat and muscular, with big pointy ears. I used to watch them lounging in the sun. They didn't look real. More like pre-Columbian statues carved out of stone.

VR

Mexico seems to have left a profound impression on you.

DELACROIX

The Aztecs were fond of their dogs, you know. They also ate them.

VR

You should finish your memoir. People would be so much more receptive now.

DELACROIX

That's a load of crap. And you know it. Change the subject, please.

VR

Did you always know you were going to be a writer?

DELACROIX

As much as any child knows anything. Or dreams about wanting to *be* something. I was passionate about books. Always asked for them at Christmas. Luckily, I was indulged. My parents—my father, especially—took pride in the fact that I was so brainy and quiet. I never gave them trouble. Until I announced my taste for women, that is. And then . . . Well, you know it was plays that made me really want to be a writer. I began by writing bad imitations of Tennessee Williams, Ibsen, and—oh, my God yes—*Lillian Hellman.*

VR

What about novels you read while you were growing up?

DELACROIX

I had access to only what was acceptable to my father. Which wasn't too awful for me, since he was an educated man and an avid reader. . . . So was my poor stoned mother, actually. Novels provided her with much-needed escape, until her eyes went from bad to worse and she had to stop reading. My parents had a kooky library. The Bible (of course), some Shakespeare, some Dickens, Pearl Buck, Ayn Rand, Thurber, John O'Hara.

VR

No Hemingway?

DELACROIX

Absolutely not! My father probably didn't approve of his politics or carousing. Could've been worse. The O'Hara books were placed on the highest shelf, since they were considered racy. Of course I snuck off to read them. At Mills I devoured Virginia Woolf, Gide, Borges—all that highfalutin shit. The surrealists, Simone de Beauvoir, ooh-la-la!

VR

Inspiring?

DELACROIX

Intimidating, intoxicating. Filled me with insatiable lust.

VR

Lust?

DELACROIX

Wanderlust. Could not wait to fucking get out of the U.S. and see the world. Thought that's what writers were supposed to do. Thought I'd end up living my life in Argentina or Paris or Tangier.

VR

But here you are. Living your life in New York.

DELACROIX

The butchers are gone. And I don't mean to sound nostalgic for the good ol' days of *Paris Is Burning*, but soon I will be, too.

VR

But you will show up to your reading at Volga, we hope?

(With great effort Delacroix rises from the sofa. She proceeds to gather our coats and show us to the door.)

DELACROIX

Sorry, kids. All this talk has drained the life out of me.

the INTERVIEW,

Part Two

We returned early the next evening and—to our delight and surprise—were greeted at the door by Delacroix's neighbor, the filmmaker Mimi Smith. Smith bade farewell to Delacroix by kissing her on both cheeks, then made a hasty exit without bothering to introduce herself. Delacroix was again barefoot and dressed in the mirrored caftan that she had on the night before. Unlike the previous evening, this time Delacroix was not as eager to see us and seemed disoriented and preoccupied.

—Sasha Collins and Rajiv Gill, 2009

VR

Yesterday you referred to writing as "exquisite agony."

DELACROIX

Must've been high. Don't trust anything I say that's too pretty and poetic.

VR

So it's not agony?

DELACROIX

For fuck's sake, of course it is! What was it that bitch Hemingway said—"Writing's not for sissies"? Novels inflict the most pain.

VR

What made you decide that *Little Deaths* had to be written as a novel?

DELACROIX

Because I'm drawn to pain. *Chantrea.*

VR

Chantrea?

DELACROIX

That was our Khmer host and translator's name. Means "moon."

VR

Oh, yes. Your time in Cambodia.

DELACROIX

There's a photograph of her in my study. Make sure her name's spelled correctly.

VR

We will.

DELACROIX

I was up all night, trying to remember her name. You think Chantrea might be dead?

VR

You want us to try to find out for you?

DELACROIX

I've never forgotten her face.

VR

Speaking of names and faces, was that Mimi Smith who opened your door?

DELACROIX

Smith's an alias.

VR

An *alias*?

DELACROIX

Mimi's an orphan. From some faraway kingdom where everyone can sing and genius lies in mimicry. Didn't speak a word of English when she got here. Taught herself by going to the movies. Or so she says.

VR

Is she aware you're giving her the film rights to *Little Deaths*?

DELACROIX

Am I? That's news to me.

VR

Last night you said—

DELACROIX

She doesn't even have a green card.

VR

This is starting to feel like one of your novels. Or *Alice in Wonderland*.

DELACROIX

There's nothing left to eat. Or drink. Everything's gone. The floors are made of glass.

VR

Are you okay? We can reschedule this interview.

DELACROIX

I never should've agreed to do this.

VR

How about tomorrow?

DELACROIX

It's over. The end.

VR

But there's so much more we—

DELACROIX

We're done.

VR

One last thing. Please, Ms. Delacroix.

DELACROIX

Shoot.

VR

Do you write for yourself?

DELACROIX

Yes.

VR

Readers be damned?

DELACROIX

Baby, it's like sex. If I can please myself . . . then maybe, just maybe, I can please *you*.

God & Smoke & Amber

The fawning pair from the magazine are finally gone, the locks in place, peace at last. Sasha and Rajiv. Such pretty names, such pretty young people. Eleanor lights a cigarette, looks around for something to drink, maybe a side of blow. Maybe not. Enough with the catnaps and nodding out. She needs sleep, real sleep. Her mind a sheet of glass, bulletproof, words cut and paste, flung into a void. She has glass on the mind, cannot shake the trite metaphor, didn't she allude to glass floors in that asinine interview? Waste of time, why had she agreed to it, no legacy. O vanity. *Mea culpa, mea culpa, mea maxima culpa.*

What injustices has she observed, what death, the long-haired kids in the temple ruins, the trembling soldiers who were kids themselves, green eyes, black stools, shroud of Yvonne, pain of the world. Eleanor suddenly cannot stop thinking about her mother. Ana Rosario Vargas. Losing ground, spinning fast, flames. Family = Aunt Elly, Mom, Pop, Petey, Nate, Richard, Jesus, Joseph, Mary. Tomorrow she'll Google the one remaining Hawthorne sibling, see what comes up. *Mary's still the baby, and she's still alive.*

Hallelujah. She finds the dusty bottle of mezcal in the back of the liquor cabinet. It's down to the dregs, but there's enough left for a buzz and a good dream. Mezcal tastes of God and smoke and amber, she remembers

Felix once saying. And he was right. Eleanor sucks it straight from the bottle. When there is no more mezcal, Eleanor goes to her bedroom and lies down. Sounds of clattering heels and laughter from the sidewalk below her window. Followed by abrupt, blessed silence. Eleanor closes her eyes and wonders in what language she will dream.

Felix Montoya waits for her at the basketball court on Horatio and Hudson. He sits on a bench by the sidelines, a forlorn king wrapped in a ragged cloak of moth-eaten jaguar pelts. His hair is plastered to his skull with blood and chicken feathers. One side of his face is gone, but he is in a jovial, playful mood. *Oye, bruja*—how dare you keep me waiting? What balls!

I'm sorry, Felix.

Can you believe this weather? It feels like spring.

Eleanor sits on his lap. It's my fault you're dead.

Narcissist.

I shouldn't have stayed at Yvonne's that night.

You're lucky you did, or you'd be dead, too.

I miss you. Eleanor touches what's left of his face.

And I miss you, Felix says.

Felix reaches inside his cloak and pulls out a black-and-white notebook. *Surprise!* The notebook looks vaguely familiar, streaked with mud and grass and bits of brain matter. Felix hands it to Eleanor. I want you to be the first to read it.

Eleanor opens to the first page.

Read it out loud. Please, Eleanor. I love the sound of your voice.

Eleanor turns to another page.

Read as loud as you want. We're all alone.

But there's nothing here, Eleanor says, flipping through the endless pages.

Exactly, Felix says. He points to the side of his face that is missing. I was three lines away from finishing the last poem in my new collection, but love got in the way.

You mean a hammer, says Eleanor, getting off his lap. She walks to the center of the court and reads from the notebook:

A hammer got in the way.
I shouldn't have left my tools out on the table.
The hammer makes everything inevitable,
Too easy.
The night air hot and sweet.
The city asleep,
Stench of marigolds.
A thousand invisible birds sing in the trees,
Calling my name.
Surprise!
The hammer comes down with a bang,
Calling my name.
It comes down
Again and again.
I love you, it sings.
Surprise! Surprise!

What a brilliant performance. Really, *bruja.* You've outdone yourself. Made a so-so poem sound much better. Felix applauds, throws his head back and laughs. His head snaps off and bounces, then rolls across the basketball court and comes to a rest against the wire fence beyond. Eleanor runs to fetch it. She runs fast. She is not herself, she is young and agile, a marathon runner, an Aztec soccer player with short, thick, powerful legs, sprinting toward the head of her friend, Felix Montoya. She reaches his head and kicks it. The court keeps expanding. She kicks it again. Felix's head sails through the sweet night air. Eleanor wakes with a start. The room is pitch black. It takes a moment for her to realize her legs are still moving.

Serve & Volley

Dashiell's face did not light up when he spotted Mimi standing in the lobby of 33/33 (aka City Arts Resource Center, 33 West Thirty-third Street). Mimi maintained a neutral expression, as if they saw each other every day, as if neither of them shared a history or a child. She was relieved that Dash was by himself when he stepped out of the elevator. She was in no mood for another awkward encounter with Paula, Dashiell's boss, or the latest earnest young intern he might be fucking. Dash looked tired and crabby, ready for a fight. Is this about Violet or money? Nice to see you, too, Mimi said. Got time for a quick drink? She was surprised when he said yes.

He took her to a garish sports bar near Penn Station. The place was crowded with people like themselves, desperate for that first drop of alcohol to kick in and flatten out the edges. Dash ordered two doubles of Jameson's neat. Mimi thinking she should really insist on wine; the whiskey was dangerous territory. But she didn't. They slipped into the only unoccupied booth and didn't say a word until the drinks came. Neither one of them took off their coats, prepared for the worst.

Mimi spoke first. Interesting, that retro goatee thing you've got going on.

Dash raised an eyebrow and kept drinking. Glad you like it.

I do. Really.

How's the new movie coming along?

On hold. Money fell through. Ivan and Matthieu— You remember Ivan, don't you?

Dash shrugged.

Well, anyway. They've both, like, *vanished.* I don't think they were who they said they were.

Too bad. Dash almost looked happy.

Mimi took a breath. I may have a new investor, but until then—I'm gonna need you to loan me some money.

Dash reared his head in mock surprise. Mimi Smith is asking *me* for a loan?

Not a lot, don't worry.

Why don't you ask Bobby? He's a dealer. Must have plenty of loose cash lying around.

Fuck off.

Dash was on a roll. Oh, yeah. I heard Bobby's dead. Is he dead?

Mimi made a move to get up. Dash grabbed her arm and gave her a pleading look. She sat back down.

Sorry about that.

Forget it, Mimi said.

Who's the new investor?

Eleanor.

Eleanor, Dash repeated. The crazy writer. She's a big fan of yours.

Mimi resisted the bait. The money I need? It's for Violet. She needs her own bed. And some other . . . you know, stuff.

I'll do what I can. Things are tight. Paula says more cuts are anticipated. I may not have a job next year.

Paula will never let them lay you off.

It's not her decision to make, Dash said. It's the board of trustees' decision.

Yeah? Mimi rolled her eyes. Then she said, Know what? Maybe it's time to go back to being an artist. Don't you miss it?

She was sticking her neck out by being sincere, and Dash let her have it.

An *artist*. Gimme a break. A little too late for that, don't you think?

Mimi was silent.

I'm moving to Fort Greene. Buying an apartment, Dash said, finishing his drink. There. He'd said it.

Mimi tensed. Then she laughed in disbelief. You can*not* be serious. *Fort Greene?* You just said money was tight.

My credit's good. Not like yours.

Mimi ignored the dig. Paula moving in with you?

She's happily married to a nice man with money, which you seem to have forgotten.

That's never gotten in your way.

Dash squelched an impulse to lean across the table and either smack Mimi or give her a kiss. He signaled for another round. Paula loves your work. She's always loved your work. Why you being such a hater? You've always been a fuckin' hater. Maybe I don't want my kid living with a *hater.*

Violet's made her decision. Can we try to work this out? For Violet's sake. Mimi glared at Dash.

I'm impressed at how mature you suddenly sound, Dash said with a smarmy smile.

Must be the mother in me.

It's very compelling, Dash said.

Now he was trying to flirt.

Advantage, Mimi. The drinks came just in time. Mimi nursed her Jameson's, determined to stay sober. Dash gazed at her while he drank. It was a gaze that Mimi knew too well, filled with anger, resentment, and longing. She felt vaguely aroused by his passion, but mostly she felt sad. Thinking as she gazed back at him, This movie sucks.

You hungry? Dash asked, trying to sound casual. It's pub food, but the shepherd's pie's pretty good.

Mimi no longer cared. It's the baby-sitter, isn't it? *Cheryl the baby-sitter.*

Oh, for fuck's sake.

She's going halfsies with you on the apartment. Doesn't the baby-sitter come from old money? She went to Bennington or Sarah Lawrence, didn't she?

Stop it.

I could've sworn she said Sarah Lawrence.

Cheryl's written a novel, Dash said in a quiet voice.

Is she calling it *Adventures in Babysitting*? A cheap shot, but Mimi couldn't help herself.

Ace. Mimi continued to nurse her drink. Dash ordered another Jameson's for himself. His face was flushed and crumbling; he was starting to slur his words.

You wanna get back together? Is that what this is about?

No, Mimi answered.

We could go to couples therapy.

Don't be ridiculous. That shit doesn't work, Mimi said.

Then why rag on me about who I'm fucking or living with?

I'm a hater, Mimi said.

The lights in the bar were too bright. The ESPN channel was too loud. Mimi tried to remain calm as she dug into her bag for her wallet. Inside the wallet were a five and a twenty. I'll come with Violet this weekend to pick up her stuff, Mimi said. Saturday around noon okay with you? Dash didn't respond. I want you to be happy, Mimi said. She threw the twenty on the table before leaving.

Bodhisattva

She showed up at Wanda Fontaine's door without an appointment, prepared to be turned away. Bobbito opened the door. Mimi broke out the smiles and good cheer. *'Sup, Bobbito?* The chunky eight-year-old boy stared back in astonishment. You've gotten so—Mimi was going to say *big* but decided against it—*tall.* Gonna let me in or what? Bobbito led her to the living room, a jungle of potted plants and mirrors, assorted *santos* and *vírgenes,* framed diplomas, blinking Christmas lights. An ornate white cage in the shape of a cathedral housed Wanda's rambunctious parrot, a Congo African gray named Lázaro. The bird began bobbing and tilting his head, sensing Mimi's presence. The apartment smelled of fried meat and Wanda's homemade shampoo-conditioner, a potent blend of avocado, lime juice, tequila, and floral extract. Wanda called it Guacamole for the Head.

The room was filled with her clients. Women waiting to have their hair done and their fortunes told, waiting to purchase medicinal brews or to order one of Wanda's three-tiered coconut cakes for a special occasion. A couple of teenage mamas were busy trying to quiet the small, bored children squirming on their laps. There was nowhere left for Mimi to sit. She leaned against a wall and stared at Wanda's television. She had to smile. Wanda, eclectic and idiosyncratic as ever, had the Tennis Channel on.

The grueling, glorious final match at Wimbledon between Nadal and Federer was in rerun. Yum, Mimi thought. In a crouch, ready for Federer's serve, Nadal tugged nervously at a wedgie. That's one big, fine ass, one of the teenage mamas couldn't resist saying. Brolic! Rafa's brolic! the other mama hooted. Fine ass! Brolic! Lázaro squawked. Rafa! Rafa! Everyone in the room burst out laughing.

Wanda paid no attention to the laughter and continued rinsing out Dinora Blanco's freshly dyed hair in the kitchen sink. Bobbito poked his head in the doorway. Pop's girlfriend's here. His grandmother looked at him sharply, then went on with her work.

Mimi—Bobbito started to say in a louder voice.

I hear you. Wanda was not pleased and made no effort to mask her annoyance.

What should I do?

Tell her to sit. Wait her turn.

There's nowhere for her to sit, Nana.

Then let her stand, Wanda snapped.

The sudden harshness in Wanda's voice startled Dinora Blanco, who was already tense. Bobbito knew not to cross Wanda further and left quickly. Wanda turned the water off. Dinora Blanco sat up. Wanda began blow-drying Dinora's hair. You can pay Bobbito on your way out, Wanda said when she was finished.

May I ask you something, please, señora?

If you're strapped, I can give you a discount. Just remember that next time I may not be so generous, Wanda said brusquely. Timid, ingratiating types like Dinora got on her nerves. She didn't trust them.

Thank you for your kind offer, señora. No need for a discount, that's not what I was going to ask, but thank you, thank you.

Enough with the thank-yous, Dinora. I have other customers waiting. ASK!

Dinora pointed to her head of brilliant copper curls. Think this color's too bright for a woman my age? I'm turning fifty-five.

Trust me, Dinora. Life is too short. The brighter, the better, Wanda said.

Wanda Fontaine was a resourceful woman of many talents and sidelines, renowned as a hairdresser and a cook, revered as a healer and a seer. She could read auras, cowrie shells, tarot cards, coffee grounds, tea leaves, the palms of people's hands, and, most disconcertingly, their faces. People often made the error of referring to Wanda as a *santera,* which never ceased to amuse her. Wanda would be the first to admit that while she had been permitted to observe and participate in certain covert ceremonies and rituals, she had never officially been initiated into any religion. No animist cult, leopard-worshipping secret society, or voodoo sect could rightfully claim her. Wanda was too independent, too strong-willed to chain herself to one set of spiritual beliefs. She believed that enlightenment could be found in the most unexpected and terrible situations. She also believed in dreams and signs, in demons and angels, in the mystical power of women and animals. She lifted what was best from the *isms*—Roman Catholicism, Santeríaism, Buddhism, Hinduism, Koranism, Lukumiism, Candombleism, Judaism, Rick Warrenism, et cetera—to remix and create her own Temple of Wanda, Our Merciful Lady of the Good Death.

Bobby used to call his mother "DJ Yeye, the Original Sampler." Wanda wasn't sure how she felt about that.

A chair finally freed up. Mimi sat down with a groan of relief. She tried calling Violet's cell, which went right to voice mail. WHERE R U? Mimi texted. SLEEPOVR W KENYA @CHARLIE'S, Violet texted back. A lie, Mimi knew. Kenya's churchgoing parents absolutely did not approve of wild-boy Charlie and his loosey-goosey, unwed, celebrity mom.

It was almost ten by the time the last of Wanda's clients paid up and said their good-byes. A drowsy-looking, pajama-clad Bobbito came through the living room with a dustpan and a broom, sweeping up crumbs of goldfish crackers and flattened juice boxes. When he was done, Bobbito draped a shawl over Lázaro's cage. He paused before the television. Want me to leave it on?

Mimi shook her head.

How's it goin' at school, Bobbito?

The boy froze. Okay, I guess. Hard.

And the asthma?

Under control.

Under control? Mimi smiled.

Bobbito shrugged. Yeah. Tha's what Nana says.

I bet your grandma stays on you about getting good grades.

Bobbito gave another shrug.

It's late. Way past your bedtime, right?

Uh-huh. Bobbito started to leave the room.

Hey, I almost forgot.

The boy glanced at Mimi warily. He had Bobby's pretty hazel eyes.

Heard anything from your pops?

The boy frowned. Then he nodded and left the room.

Mimi moved to the sofa and steeled herself for Wanda. Except for the annoying Christmas lights, the room was dark and peaceful. Wanda emerged at long last from her kitchen. Mimi noticed that Bobby's mother had grown heavy and tired-looking. Wanda swayed slightly as she walked, as if the weight were too much for her knees and her heart to bear. She kicked off her slippers and settled into her dead husband's La-Z-Boy recliner, resting her swollen feet on a little stool. I don't like what I see, Wanda murmured, staring at Mimi.

Mimi didn't respond.

Is your daughter safe?

Violet's strong. Violet's fine.

Are you here about my son?

I'm lost, Mimi said.

Wanda snorted in disdain. *Lost.* It's because you don't eat. Why don't you eat? Never mind. I know the answer to that one.

If you want me to go, I'll go, Mimi said.

Not before I feed the both of us. Wanda got up with a sigh and made her way slowly back to the kitchen. A few minutes passed. Mimi heard the insistent beeping of a microwave. Lázaro, roused from sleep, imitated the beeping sounds. Get off your skinny ass and set the table, Wanda ordered Mimi in a sharp voice.

Skinny ass! Set the table! Lázaro echoed.

They sat down to a stew of pork and green chiles over yellow rice, eating in ravenous silence. When they were done, Mimi got up to wash the dishes. Wanda remained at the table, observing her intently. The faint, disturbing aura around Mimi was less evident in the drab fluorescent light. But it was definitely there, and Wanda was not fooled. When Mimi was done with the dishes, Wanda asked her to bring out a bottle and two glasses from one of the cabinets. The bottle was unlabeled, filled with dark rum. A gift, Wanda said, from a very special client. She apologized for not offering cigars to go with the rum. I quit smoking, Wanda said. She gave Mimi a hard, meaningful look. And furthermore, I no longer permit anyone to smoke *anything* in this apartment. You understand what I'm saying?

I understand, Mimi said. Her tone was respectful.

I don't have what you're looking for. Got rid of everything evil in my house when I sent my son away.

Okay, Wanda.

Okay? So. Now I need to ask *you* something.

Mimi waited.

How'd you get past security?

Mimi was baffled. Excuse me?

The guard, Wanda said. He's supposed to call before letting any visitors up here. Those are the *rules*.

A digression: The formidable Wanda Fontaine lived in Building 5 of the towering projects on Ninth Avenue known as the Peter Minuit Houses. The Minuit was where Wanda and her husband, Roberto, had raised Bobby Junior and his three older sisters. The Minuit was where Wanda had watched Roberto rot away from lung and liver cancer. The Minuit was where the Widow Wanda was now raising Bobbito, Bobby's son by a high-school flame named Yessica. Yessica had moved to Miami and was no longer interested in being a mother. Bobbito's safety was of paramount concern to Wanda. In fact, safety had become one of her recent obsessions. She was one of many older tenants in the Peter Minuit Houses and was grateful that a uniformed guard sat behind a counter in the front lobby of her building 24/7. Tenants were issued laminated ID cards, and guests were required to sign in and out, no matter how many times they came to visit. It was a soul-crushing way to live, but the Widow Wanda had a practical side. She understood the necessity.

No one was in the lobby. No security guard, nothing, Mimi said.

I dreamed you were going to show up at my door. And here you are.

Mimi emptied her glass of rum.

You caused a lot of trouble for my son.

I miss him, Wanda. A lot.

Wanda spoke calmly, without anger or judgment. But you never loved him. Not the way he loved you. Not the way he loved his family.

Wanda was wrong, but Mimi didn't bother denying it.

And you never loved your husband. What's his name? He had a funny name.

Dashiell. We weren't married.

If you have a baby and live with that baby's father, then you are married, Wanda said. You know what I said to *my* husband after Junior brought you here to meet us? "That girl has bad karma."

Mimi made a wan attempt at sarcasm. Gee, Wanda. Thanks.

I see what I see. I know what I know. And— What do you people say?

Call it like it is.

Wanda gave a raucous laugh and poured another round. The rum tasted like burning sugarcane fields. Mimi felt the heat coursing through her body. If only she could smoke. Like in the old days, when she and Bobby would drop by to check in on his newly widowed, insomniac mother. They'd hang out all night, smoking and drinking and listening to Wanda's rambling, grief-stricken monologues.

You believe in karma?

Yes, unfortunately, Mimi answered.

Why unfortunately? You gotta quit being so negative, girl. Check it out. I shouldn't be drinking because of my diabetes. But in moderation, a little vice can't hurt. Right? Moderation and a positive outlook. That's the key. You understand what I'm saying?

Absolutely. Inwardly Mimi was alarmed by Wanda's Oprah-esque pronouncements. It wasn't like Wanda to be maudlin and trite. Mimi hadn't come all the way up to the sixteenth floor of Building 5 of the Peter Minuit Houses for a touchy-feely lecture on sobriety and moderation. From Bobby's mother, no less.

A lot of people think Bobby's dead, Mimi said. I'm starting to think maybe he is.

I sent my son home, Wanda said. Where I know he'll be *safe.* You ever think of going home?

New York is home, Mimi said. Fucked up as it is. Fucked up as I am. Why are you still here, Wanda?

I ask myself that every day, Wanda said.

It was time. Wanda closed her eyes and placed both hands flat on the table. Her voice grew heavy and dark as the lovely rum they were drinking, rum not from Cuba but from the abyss of Haiti or maybe

Guatemala. You hurry into the empty lobby of my building, Wanda said. The guard's chair lays across the floor. Blood splattered everywhere, even on the walls. But this doesn't surprise you. The elevators are out of order. This doesn't surprise you either. You climb the stairs to the sixteenth floor, open the door into a little room. Wanda's dark, heavy voice changed into the brighter voice of a young girl. You see a small bowl made of tin sitting on a shelf. The bowl is filled with gravy, gravy yellow and thick as wax. You hear rats chirping and scratching behind the walls of the room. Children screaming for their mothers. The children are trapped inside the walls. You hear them trying to claw their way out. You dip a spoon (it just appears!) into the waxy yellow liquid. Tilt your head sideways and pour the boiling yellow wax (which doesn't hurt you) into your right ear. Straighten your head and look in the mirror. The pain is gone. Everything stops. Wanda made strange faces and moved her head, as if listening for something. Mimi stared at the old woman, riveted. The children. The rats. Everything suddenly silent. Then comes the roar of the bitter ocean. Wanda's voice changed back into her own. *Bitter ocean,* Wanda repeated, which Mimi misheard as "Bitter Oshun." Orisha of love, motherhood, beauty, mirrors, vanity, love, et cetera! Whose color is yellow, the color of madness and daffodils, yellow like the waxy gravy in Wanda's dream.

You dive into the bitter ocean, Wanda murmured. Hoping to find your mother in the bottomless deep. Hoping to find your father. Hoping to find someone else who is lost, covered with branches and leaves.

Mimi couldn't resist correcting her. You're wrong. My parents didn't drown, Wanda. A bomb blew up in the market, killing everyone there.

Wanda's eyes stayed closed. Her face serene and unperturbed, almost beautiful. She drew a deep breath and smiled. Her voice became young again, plaintive and high-pitched. How long must I wait to be found? The forest is lonely, Wanda moaned. Lonely. Lonely. Lonely.

Holy Thursday

The washing of feet, the last supper, the reading at Volga. She would finish writing *her new piece,* throbbing arthritic fingers be damned. Strange how excited she felt. She did not have a title for it yet. But she wasn't worried. "Untitled" was her back-up, and it always worked. Whether "Untitled" ended up being some sort of condensed narrative of her life or someone else's, some sort of elegy or confession or manifesto, some sort of dream or poem, didn't really matter. Strange, exciting, *new.* What was it young Violet had said to her the other night? *You go, Eleanor.* And still the option of not showing up at the bar remained a distinct possibility. Looming like the shadow of death or maybe the shadow of a serpentine jaguar on the horizon of her ever-diminishing possibilities. It would have been nice to have birthed a child, someone to whom Eleanor could bestow her—

~

Thank God she got Vukocevic's voice mail. Alex? Mimi. Look. I don't mean to be a bitch or anything, but I think— I mean, you're a lovely person, the way you took care of me and my animal, I was touched, I mean that, really mean that, okay? It's just . . . I am not ready to go out with you or with anyone else, I am not ready for all this attention. You've left me, like, *eleven* messages since we met, for fuck's sake, Alex! It's better if you stop calling me, okay? You're a beautiful man, but. Please. STOP.

~

They were lying on his bed staring up at the undulating ocean of Charlie's ceiling, stoned on the last of her father's mushrooms, listening to Rufus Wainwright really loud. (Too loud, Violet thought. Why couldn't Charlie put on Wild Beasts or Lil Wayne?) Blair says Obama's a sellout, Charlie said. No way, Violet said. Your mom said *that*? Blair says all that *sí, se puede* stuff was a load of crap, Charlie continued. That Obama's really a centrist and she's sorry she ever volunteered for his campaign. Nothing's going to change, Charlie said. That's not true, said Violet. Blair thinks you're pretty, Charlie said. She thinks Kenya's pretty, too, but Blair—and here Charlie gave a little goofy laugh—thinks you're *really* pretty. Violet remembered she had Wild Beasts on her iPod. Blair likes when you spend the night, Charlie said. Ewww, Violet said. Like maybe someday we'll give her grandchildren or something, Charlie said. That'll be the day, Violet murmured. Inwardly she was thrilled. Actually, the mushrooms made her feel like her heart was bursting, like she could fly right up to the sky. Blair knows you're queer, right? Of course she knows, Charlie said. She's my mother.

~

I'm dreaming again, Eleanor said. Jesusfuckingchrist, Eleanor! Your brain has really and truly short-circuited, Eleanor heard Yvonne saying in an impatient, contemptuous voice. Has the computer finally crashed? It will, mark my words. The cranky voice came from her study. Eleanor got up from bed, went down the hall to her study, and peered in. The desk lamp was on; so was the computer. Her eyeglasses lay on top of the printer. Eleanor went in and put on her glasses. She was anxious to read what was on the computer screen. Had she finished with her new piece? Shit. Five new e-mails in her in-box. Fourteen total, most of it spam. *E-mail.* This is how I spent my fucking time? Disgusted with herself, Eleanor sat down and signed out. She clicked open the "untitled new" file on her desktop.

~

Mimi took the 7 train to Woodside and walked the five blocks to her brother's apartment building. A note was taped to the front door: BUZZER BROKEN. Mimi called Carmelo on her cell. I'm downstairs. A few minutes went by before Carmelo appeared at the front door. His eyes were bloodshot, and he had a wild look about him, like he hadn't slept for days. Mimi detected the faint stink of bourbon as she followed him up the stairs to his apartment. They found a woman's body in the woods, Carmelo said. Out in Jersey. A detective called me. They think it's Agnes. They need us to go out there and make a positive ID. Mimi made a place for herself on the cluttered futon sofa. It's Agnes, Mimi said. I know it. *You know it?* Carmelo ran a hand through his long, unkempt hair, which stuck out in all directions. Dreams, Mimi said.

~

Violet was almost as infatuated with Blair Dalton as she was with her son. Blair was a renowned stage actress, fabulous and mercurial. She did plays by Euripides, Beckett, and Tony Kushner. Charlie liked to brag about his mother's Obie Awards (three) and Tony nominations (one). Blair called acting "my craft" and was a snob about it. She did not do lighthearted musicals or comedies. She did not do movies. "Hollywood has no interest in females over the age of puberty," Blair once said in an interview in *Interview.* For some reason she had no problems with television. She had guest-starred on *Law & Order* (a lot), *The L Word,* and *Sex and the City* (twice), and *The Sopranos* (once). *The Sopranos* was a very big deal. Violet's parents were still together then; Violet remembers staying up to watch with them. Blair hardly had any lines, but she had a sex scene and died memorably at the hands of James Gandolfini. Violet remembers how the gruesome episode made her cry. You know how my mother gets when she's drunk, Charlie said. Thinking everyone's pretty. Pretty, pretty, pretty, Charlie kept repeating. He had moved on to snorting coke. Are you inferring I'm not pretty? Violet asked, indignant. You mean *implying,* Charlie said. The person listening—meaning me—is the one who *infers* a meaning from what the person speaking *implies.* Meaning you, Violet. Violet watched Charlie snort another line. Charlie and his coke and his boring Rufus Wainwright music were really getting on her nerves. You are so fucking *officious* and *condescending* and *OCD,* Violet said. And *pretty,* Charlie said. Don't forget pretty.

~

Why not leave her literary estate to Mimi? That would be a hoot. Besides, there was no one left in Eleanor's life. Well, maybe Benjamin. Of course, Benjamin. Benjy, Nneka, and the beautiful baby who was about to be born. There would be justice in leaving everything to them, but . . . *Mimi.* True, it was all a bit perverse, what with Eleanor making love to her just the other night. But that would happen once and only once. Which is more than enough for this old writer, Eleanor thinks grimly.

~

You gonna offer me something to drink? Mimi asked. Carmelo shrugged. Yeah, sure. Why not? He sauntered into the tiny room where he slept and came back with a half-empty bottle of Maker's Mark. Don't worry, Carmelo said, disappearing into the kitchen. There's another bottle. He returned with two clean glasses. Here we go, he said. Mimi did the honors and handed her brother a drink. So what happened? she asked him. Guess I fell into the deep blue sea, Carmelo said. Mimi's laugh was soft and knowing. Well, she sighed. Who am I to judge? I'm renting a car, Carmelo said. Told the detective we'd go out there in the morning. Frank's her fucking father, Mimi said. Why can't *he* get on a fucking plane and identify Agnes's body? Uncle Frank's had a stroke, Carmelo said. That's why I've been trying to reach you. He was in the ICU at Kaiser, but he's home now. How convenient, Mimi said.

~

Violet watched the ceiling burst open, radiating phosphorescent light. Or maybe water. Or Devi's billowing skirt of mirrors. We're under the sea or in heaven, Violet thought. She felt the urge to write a poem. She turned and kissed Charlie on the lips, startling the boy with the depth and ferocity of her longing.

~

Eleanor's decision to stop having anything more to do with doctors had everything to do, as you may already have guessed, with watching Yvonne grow sick and sicker and finally, and blessedly, die. Eleanor was not a fan of doctors. She found them lacking in wisdom, humor, empathy, style, and compassion. The only exception was Dr. Sheila Singh, an Oxford-trained geriatric specialist who was Eleanor's personal physician. The last time Eleanor went to her for a checkup was four years ago. I am pleased to say that you are in robust health for a woman of your age, Dr. Singh had said in that clipped and coiffed, snotty, queen-of-England accent of hers that Eleanor so loved. You've got to be kidding, Sheila, Eleanor responded, genuinely surprised. She was not sure whether to laugh or cry. No, Eleanor. I absolutely am not, Dr. Singh said. Although I am absolutely *not* pleased by the traces of cocaine found in your blood and urine samples. Aren't you a bit too old for this sort of stuff?

~

Wanda lifted the shawl and peered inside the cage. Lázaro, who was, in parrot years, as old as Wanda was, rustled his feathers and stared back at her with eyes full of love. Good night, Guapito, Wanda said, blowing the parrot a kiss. Lázaro shifted from one foot to another. *Wanda, Wanda, Wanda.* On the way to her bedroom, Wanda checked on Bobbito. The frowning boy lay fast asleep with a thumb in his mouth. It was a habit eight-year-old Bobbito hadn't outgrown yet, like he hadn't outgrown wetting the bed. Habits that used to bother Bobby when he was still around, Bobby who sweated over his son's masculinity too damn much, in Wanda's opinion. So what if the boy sucked his thumb, made pee-pee on the bed, had nightmares, and liked playing with girls more than boys? Wanda bought a plastic undersheet to protect the mattress on Bobbito's bed, and that was that. She kept reminding Bobby that he should be thankful for his son. Wanda would always see to it that Bobbito felt safe, that he *was* safe. She left the night-light on and the door ajar, in case Bobbito had a bad dream. Wanda proceeded down the dark hall to her own room. The half-blind cat and the three-legged mutt Wanda had rescued from extermination snuggled together on her bed. The animals raised their heads as soon as she walked in. Wanda could have sworn the cat was smiling.

~

Eleanor stared at the computer screen. It's all there, Yvonne said in that loud, grating voice, making her jump. You're done. Get dressed and make your grand exit, baby. Eleanor did not turn around, but she could smell the fecund scent of Yvonne's signature perfume, dark and green and humid like a forest.

Somnambulant Ballad

I can't look at her, Mimi said, pushing away the crime scene photograph. After a pause, Carmelo spoke. Let me, he said. He gazed at the close-up of a woman's face in black and white. Eyes closed (had the state troopers done that for their benefit?), slack-mouthed. Faint hint of scar. I'm not sure, Carmelo said, handing the digital print back to Detective Carmen Banks. It's been a while since— Carmelo blinked several times and swallowed hard. He was trying not to crumble.

Your cousin was killed somewhere else, Detective Banks said. Then her body was dumped in the woods. You ready to hear this? Carmelo nodded. Mimi sat slumped in the metal folding chair next to his, her face devoid of emotion. Banks thinking, Funny pair. The tense, awkward brother doing most of the talking, the sister remote, vaguely hostile. They had shown up at the state police headquarters earlier that morning without calling ahead. Sergeant Dempsey, sweaty and frazzled, escorted them upstairs to Banks's cluttered office. Next of kin, Dempsey had announced. Or something like that. Banks gave Dempsey a look but decided not to push it. She'd been savoring her second mug of been-on-the-burner-too-long shitty black coffee when they walked in. Coffee, especially *black* coffee, was high on her doctor's list of things to avoid, but Banks couldn't imagine a day without consuming at least five cups.

Who found her? Carmelo asked.

Couple of locals on a hike. She was—Banks almost used the word *stuffed* but caught herself—placed inside a bag before being left in the—

What kind of bag?

Laundry. One of those big ones.

Mimi found the little memo pad buried in the bottom of her own bag. The cop's desk was a fascinating mess. Mimi wrote:

sad orangutan hanging from tree (desktop image on computer)

folders/papers

"I ❤ Vermont" mug w/ BIC pens & Sharpies

small repro statue of Egyptian cat deity Bastet/ goddess of joy/ protector of women oval candy dish jelly beans/ M & M's

Here we go, Mimi thought. Fucking women with their sweet-tooth-and-cat thing. She smiles brightly for Banks. Mind if I use one of your pens?

Go right ahead, Banks said. You a reporter or what?

My sister's a— Carmelo began.

The notes are strictly for me, Mimi said. So I don't forget. That's not forbidden or illegal, is it?

Detective Banks was unfazed by Mimi's attempt at provocation. Nope. Take all the notes you want. I'll get you a copy of the police report when we're done.

Carmelo jumped in before Mimi could say another word. We're not done, but thank you for being so kind and helpful, Detective Banks.

a's body, stuffed into a 30" x 40" nylon laundry bag, dumped across tracks of abandoned railroad by Paulinskill River. Lacerations on . . .

You know the Paulinskill?

No, Carmelo said. Imagining Agnes curled up in a laundry bag.

Paulinskill's like—again the motherly detective in search of the precise word—part of the Delaware River. It's really very interesting, the history of this place. I'm not from around here. Always thought of New Jersey as kinda— Banks paused. Why was she telling them this? The sister stops scribbling and stares at Banks with great curiosity. I dunno, Banks said. A cliché about Jersey being a nothing kinda state, I guess.

Where you from? Not that Carmelo cared, but he knew to be polite and ask.

New Hampshire, Banks answered proudly.

Mimi kept her head down as she scribbled away in the little notebook. What the hell was she writing? Banks wondered.

Ask about the body, Mimi said to Carmelo.

My sister— Carmelo began.

I'd say a bear, Banks said.

Mimi stopped writing and looked up.

The bear, Banks explained, had ripped the purportedly tear-resistant nylon laundry bag to shreds and dragged away parts of the body deep into the brush. To devour in seclusion, Banks continued, after a brief silence in which Carmelo and Mimi gazed back at her with stunned eyes. Bears are usually shy, omnivorous creatures, Banks said. Then she said, I'm sorry.

Mimi decided that the motherly detective was embarrassed, ashamed by something. Was it her geeky knowledge of animal lore and evident sympathies? Mimi fantasized excusing herself for a quick detour to the women's restroom down the hall, where she could lock herself in one of the toilet stalls for a bump or two. Or swallow a Dilaudid. But the

New Jersey State Police probably had surveillance cameras installed in the restrooms. She then fantasized a bracing shot of mezcal and a cigarette. It was 11:22 in the morning. The wounds on her arm were itching and her bandages needed to be changed. The motherly detective was talking again. Apparently, what parts of Agnes the bear left behind were first covered with dirt, broken branches, and leaves.

Sign of respect by the animal, Carmelo supposed.

Yeah, Banks said. Bears do that.

The alleged black bear, Mimi said, her laugh curt and bitter. The *perp.*

You okay, miss? asked Banks.

How do you know it was a bear? You don't have witnesses, evidence!

Shut up, for fuck's sake, Carmelo said.

Why? Mimi glowered at her brother. Why should I shut up?

It occurred to Carmen Banks that the sniffling, erratic younger woman sitting across from her desk had probably stuffed something powerful up her nose before heading out to New Jersey. Maybe the brother, too. Maybe today wouldn't be so boring and predictable after all. There were bear droppings, Banks said to Mimi in a gentle voice. Around the area where the remains of the deceased were found. That's evidence enough for me.

You're an animal lover, Mimi said.

Yes, ma'am. I most certainly am.

~

They leaned against the rental car, brother and sister in a state of mild shock. Mimi held the nine-by-twelve envelope close to her chest. Inside were three copies of the police report and Detective Banks's business card. On the back Banks had written her cell-phone number. Just in case, Banks had said. She shook hands with both Carmelo and Mimi as a way of saying good-bye.

Carmelo had parked the Nissan Versa in the lot next to the state police station, a three-story concrete affair adjacent to a drab strip mall off the highway. Nails R Us, Hi-Way Liquors, Rite Aid, Subway, Dunkin' Donuts, 7-Eleven, Hallmark. The usual purveyors of drabness and treacle. Yet the sun was out and it was one of those brisk, radiant days. Mimi wondered if they'd run into traffic heading back to Manhattan. She had a phobia about sitting in traffic, based on nothing at all. She liked blaming her anxiety on Godard's *Weekend*. It was her favorite Godard movie, the only one that she could still bear to watch after all these years. Certain images were indelible, yet filtered over time they had become Mimi's own version of the film. The endless violent traffic jam, the saucer of milk, the woman with blond hair perched on the kitchen counter, the band of hippie cannibal musicians, the tedious, hypnotic drum solo played over a white-hot screen. The poem about the ocean. She first saw *Weekend* when she was Violet's age. Fourteen years old. Mimi had cut school to meet up with Julian, who was middle-aged, married, and paid her to sleep with him. Julian dabbled in photography and real estate and always had plenty of money. He owned a beat-up Porsche and liked driving to San Francisco to eat foreign food and watch foreign movies. Let's check out the Godard festival at the Roxie, Mimi remembers him saying. Whatever. As long as you get me back to Colma in time, Mimi had said. She remembers him laughing. *But of course, my dear.* They were walking toward his car. Julian looked around to make sure no one could see him, then grabbed her taut, perfect little ass and gave it a squeeze.

Now, at the far end of the parking lot, two crows were going at it on the uppermost branches of a red oak tree. The birds pecked wildly at each other, their squawking ugly and shrill. Mimi wasn't sure if they were fighting or fucking, but she was transfixed. She lit a cigarette.

Gimme a smoke, Carmelo said.

What am I, your enabler? Mimi snickered, handing him the pack of American Spirits. The smaller of the two crows flapped its bloodied wings and flew off to safety. The other preened and strutted on the tree branch, cawing in triumph.

Carmelo took a deep drag and punched in Frank's number on his cell. Frank's ancient voice croaked something like hello.

Uncle Frank? You need to come out here.

Carmelo?

You need—

The old man made choking sounds. *They found her???*

It's bad, Carmelo said. Is—Carmelo hated saying her name—Evie there with you? You shouldn't be alone.

Nobody. Frank wheezing and sobbing. Nobody's here.

Mimi decides she wants to hear the old man grovel. She tugged on her brother's sleeve. Put him on speakerphone, she whispered. Carmelo frowned but did as he was told. He took another hit off the cigarette before speaking. You're her father, Uncle Frank. Mimi and I have no authority. You're the one who's supposed to deal with all this . . . *stuff.*

I just got out of the hospital, Frank said. I'm sick.

Sick old bastard, Mimi muttered, loud enough for Carmelo to hear.

Can't travel, Frank whined. Doctor's orders. Asthma, diabetes, psoriasis, my heart—you name it, I got it. They did a biopsy the other day. Found a lump in my—

Agnes was beaten to death. Or maybe she killed herself by banging her own head against a wall. One thing for sure—they left her body in the woods. Carmelo spit out the words, wanting to inflict pain.

Who's they? What the cops have to say? Frank's tone was guarded and no longer pitiful. You tell them how to find me? Don't tell them anything.

Mimi couldn't stand it any longer and grabbed the cell from Carmelo. She was a slave! They left her in the woods! A bear ate parts of her body! Don't you fucking even give a shit?

The old man fell to sobbing again. Why do you hate me so much? I took care of your brother and you when—

I'm gonna make a movie about Agnes, Mimi said. She was on fire now. I'm gonna make a horror movie about her life and everyone in it. Including *you.*

Eleanor Delacroix Has a Cold

At the appointed time, we sent a car service to pick up Delacroix in Manhattan. Volga was packed with a diverse, more-rowdy-than-usual audience that night, everyone eager to see and hear the legendary author. The reading was scheduled for 8:00 P.M. At exactly 7:45 the town car pulled up. I was waiting outside, ready to escort Delacroix into the bar. The driver opened the passenger door, and the filmmaker Mimi Smith was the first to emerge, followed by a long-legged beauty whose face looked terribly familiar. And no Eleanor Delacroix.

Needless to say, I was furious. Before I could open my mouth to ask where she was, Smith held up her hand. I'll explain when we're inside, Rajiv. Let's just go ahead and get started. We made our way through the standing-room crowd. The atmosphere was festive and full of anticipation. I went up to the podium and introduced Mimi Smith.

Eleanor Delacroix can't be here tonight, Smith said. She has a cold. She's come down with that awful bug that's been going around— Are you gonna fucking boo all night, or let me speak? Smith paused, then asked me to fetch her a shot of Patrón. Actually, Rajiv, you may as well make that a double, Smith said. And a Diet Coke for Darlene. She waited at the podium for the crowd to settle down before continuing with her dramatic introduction. Eleanor Delacroix wants you to hear a brand-new piece that she's written.

Are any of you interested, or should we just get drunk and go home?

Enough with the feeble foreplay, Mimi whoever you are! Get on with the show! a very old, hunchbacked man shouted from the bar. I don't have much time left on this piece-of-shit earth! (After Googling critic Leonard Schilling and finding out that he was still very much alive, of course I'd made sure to invite him to the Delacroix event.)

Okay, asshole, whoever *you* are, Smith responded with a smile. Moving right along. Darlene Drayton's here. Darlene starred in a little movie I made called *Blood Wedding*—maybe some of you have seen it. Anyway, Darlene's gonna read from Eleanor Delacroix's new work, so new I can't remember if it even has a title. Darlene? Come on up here, Darlene. (All hell broke loose—clapping, cheering, stomping—as the statuesque and sexy actress strode up to the podium, Diet Coke in hand.)

We never heard from Delacroix about her no-show at Volga. We were mystified and saddened by the news of her disappearance and presumed death in the days that followed. Permission to publish *Monologue of Desire* in this special issue was granted by Mimi Smith, the designated executor of Delacroix's estate.

—Rajiv Gill, 2009

Monologue of Desire

I was beautiful. Some of you went so far as to say I was possessed.

~

Even as a child, I could smell your fear and unease, your jealousy and confusion. Who and what was I? Your endless speculating about the dubious origins of my exotic looks and mystifying gender was amusing to me then and still is now. *Possibly Caucasian, possibly not.*

~

Object of desire, vain young thing of fading beauty, altar boy, sacrificial virgin, fugitive, shape-shifter. For months I eluded anxious captors, hiding in plain sight. For months I carried a gun, stolen from the lover I killed one night with a hammer. There were other things I stole from my beloved: an ancient gold coin, possibly Roman, which I later pawned; his leather jacket, which I had always coveted; one thousand U.S. dollars in cash, which came in quite handy; his manuscript of poetry, which did not.

~

Here's what made me really happy—I stole his Mercedes, which I drove across the desert without stopping to rest or eat. How long did it take? Who knows? What happened to the car? Who knows? Perhaps I left it on a side street in some rural village, the engine still running. Perhaps I doused it with gasoline and watched as it burst into flames. Who knows?

~

On a broiling day like any other day, I slip unnoticed into the desolate coliseum. The hammer and gun—a nine-millimeter Browning pistol—are artfully concealed by my dead lover's jacket. It is too hot to wear anything, but I have no choice. The hammer and gun—my props, if you will—cannot be revealed until the very end of my performance.

~

I am the first to admit: I have sinned.

I am the first to admit: I used to have style.

I am the first to admit: There was a time.

I am the first to admit: I was the chosen one, before bits of my face started falling off, before my songs became predictable, my dance no longer dazzled, and the audience—fickle audience!—got ahead of me. Before I left behind a trail of corpses.

~

Being wanted comes so easy at first. Eat like a pig, never gain a pound.

My parting words of wisdom to you: Forget substance, babe. It's about style.

~

Once upon a time, I was a little girl with a forked tongue, my head of glossy ringlets spinning like a top. My blind mother had herself nailed to a cross once a year and rose from the dead on Easter Sunday. I wore a pink flannel nightgown, avoided my father, prayed with my mother, wet the bed every night. The black dog came to me in dreams. The black dog whispered in my ear, taught me the rules of desire. The black dog leaped through the bedroom window night after night, kept my head spinning.

~

My voice changed without warning. My beard grew, and I learned to shave. There were blessings. There were curses. I began to speak in tongues. People paid to hear me growl, to see me eat fire. A born performer, they all gushed. No doubt about it.

~

At fourteen I trade the flannel nightgown for a sleek red jumpsuit. My hyena laugh doesn't quite fit the picture, but none of you seem to mind. *Life of the party.* It was uncanny, really. I always knew which name to drop and how to work the room.

⁂

Don't need the gym or the pool at first. Physique trim and tight, muscles oiled and gleaming. Without ever having to break a sweat, mind you.

⁂

Dream come true: Eat like a pig, never gain a pound.

⁂

I peaked at nineteen. But before that? Glorious. I knew what was important. I could dance and throw a punch, dive through flaming hoops and get paid.

⁂

My mother called pig *lechón*. Which I, the child, found quaint, chalking it up to some bit of faraway tropical-paradise lingo, from some faraway tropical island where—if you bought into the delicious bullshit flying fast and loose out of my blind mother's mouth—suckling pigs were slaughtered, roasted, and devoured every minute of every hot fucking delicious day.

⁂

My father leaves one morning. Goes out for cigarettes and never comes back. Next thing we know, he sells our house right out from under us. Mother gets in bed, crawls under the duvet, plucks out her own eyes, and keeps praying. Her faith is deep and bottomless. An abyss.

~

I love to get high. You remember how I was famous for my irony and biting, mordant wit when I was high; you remember my astonishing gift for mimicry. You remember how I, object of fading youth and fading beauty, always aimed to please.

~

In this quiet arena, in the center of this scorching field of red clay, I gaze at the rows of empty seats that surround me and listen hard for the roar of absent fans. Demanding, angry, excited fans. Thousands of them, millions of them. Impatient lovers and haters chanting in unison, screaming my name. Heaven.

~

I disrobe quickly, relieved to shed my rotting shoes and rotting socks, the greasy jeans and shirt I've been wearing for months. Months! Last to go are the hammer, Felix Montoya's leather jacket, and the loaded gun—*where to put the fucking loaded gun?* My bloodshot gaze wanders over to The Bed of Urine-Soaked Sheets, epicenter of an elaborate installation by the most famous writer of them all, Anonymous.

~

I love women and artists and writers, I love artists who have cunts and writers who have cunts. Don't you? I've spent hours in galleries and museums all over the world, pored over books of art history, seriously flirted with the idea of becoming a curator or a pimp. But to be an artist—

~

?

~

Define *Neverland.*

~

A glimpse of the fabulous universe I once knew: jungle, tent, telescope, dollhouse, trumpet, swimming pool, prayer book, mother, boxing gloves, needle, crucifix, tennis ball, vial, father, ruby slippers, buttons of ivory, sister, cloisonné beads, brother, lover, noose of gold thread.

~

I crawl into the damp, cold bed clutching my gun. Shall I hide it under a pillow? It's been months since I've heard applause, months since I've slept.

~

Look at these hideous hands. I feel old.

⁂

It is the middle of summer; brutal. The Aztec dogs are singing. The desolate stadium bakes in the desert sun. I drift off to a fitful sleep, lulled by the intense heat and my intense nakedness. Buzz of black flies swarming above my head. Smell of rot and dreams in which I am more wanted than ever. I dive into a black sea of broken mirrors and begin to swim.

⁂

Once upon a time, my Mother climbed down from the cross and sang me a lullaby. Once upon a time in our kitchen of Formica and linoleum, Mother baked a towering cake for my birthday. It took her all day. The kitchen became engulfed in tantalizing aromas of cardamom, butter, sweat, and burning fields of sugarcane.

⁂

Mother said, You are the chosen one.

Father once said, You are our pride and joy.

⁂

Inside this vast, ancient ruin, my childhood dream house sits on a dais near The Bed of Urine-Soaked Sheets. My house re-created as an extravagant dollhouse of a thousand and one little rooms by that wicked female artist, Anonymous. Dollhouse rooms furnished with loving attention to detail, as if to taunt me. Miniature doll portraits in baroque frames hang above the miniature fireplace; three miniature Xoloitzcuintles curled up on a bed. A mother and her pups. Books, so many miniature books, line the shelves of a windowless study. A miniature samovar filled with vodka rests on a miniature sideboard, next to a miniature tray of teeny olive and goat-cheese tarts garnished with even teenier dollops of gleaming black caviar. All so rococo and insane, this ridiculous and loving attention to detail, how can I sleep?

~

I was tall and strong for my age. Described as King Kong by some. Graceful as a ballerina by others. Pornographer and poet, nun and whore. My audience of believers grew by the hundreds, then the thousands. Then I lost faith.

~

I spoke perfect English. Fame was my vocation. It tastes like semen. Like the gleaming metal head of a hammer. Turpentine. Gunpowder. Black pellets of shit from a man's ass. The juice from a woman's cunt.

~

I love getting high. You remember how famous I was for getting high. I'd rather get high than drunk. There's a difference.

&

Do not overburden me with meaning, Anonymous once said. Or maybe it was me.

&

The Aztec dogs run in circles and howl. The door to paradise is always open.

Violet Smith

I was on my way home from school, in a really bad mood. Fuck Mr. Pavino. Fuck Charlie and Kenya. Fuck Omar and Bethanne. Fuck my period. Fuck Coco Schnabel on the sidewalk with her dumb little dog, no doubt ranting to the FedEx guy about something Mayor Bloomberg did or didn't do for the people of New York like she always does. Fuck the FedEx guy for being too nice, smiling and nodding at Coco and going uh-huh, uh-huh, uh-huh.

The people of New York. Woo-hoo. Romeo Byron showed up in my dream last night. *Très, très* weird, how the people of New York really came out for me when I died. I don't deserve it, he said. Romeo looked depressed. Really depressed, but *hot*. He leaned over and kissed me. Sweet, not like a perv or anything. Then he said, I love you, Violet. FYI.

I spotted Eleanor in the lobby. Coming out of the elevator, moving real slow. Like maybe her arthritis had spread to her knees and was acting up. She had lipstick on and was looking pretty cool. Handbag, fancy red coat, funny little boots, and this wicked hat. I held the front door open for her.

What are you listening to on that iPod of yours, Violet?

I took my earphones out and tried not to sound annoyed. Excuse me?

Eleanor pointed to her ear and smiled.

Lil Wayne, I told her.

Must be good, Eleanor said.

I had to laugh.

I was gonna offer to help her cross the street, but I didn't. Like I said, I was in a really bad mood. I watched her do it, though. Watched Eleanor Delacroix cross the street and walk up the block. It took forever. Then this fucking tree got in the way and I couldn't see her anymore.

I never told my mother.